A Hollow Throne

Andrew Clawson

Get Andrew Clawson's Starter Library FOR FREE

Sign up for the no-spam newsletter and get two novels for free.

Details can be found at the end of this book.

Prologue

August 1707
Edinburgh, Scotland

Thick clouds hovered above the castle. Sheets of rain drowned the screams coming from the single iron-barred window at ground level, scarcely large enough for a man to squeeze through. If he managed to escape. Flickering torchlight in the castle dungeon sent shadows dancing on damp walls. A man lay stretched in the room's center, arms and legs pulled in opposite directions as the rack tightened its deadly embrace. Two others watched. One of them repeated his question for the fourth time over the sound of wind whistling through the empty castle.

"Where are they?" he demanded. Blood dripped from the racked man's tongue as he grimaced. "Tell me where it is hidden and this all will end."

"Piss off."

The questioner nodded to his partner, and the rack tightened again. The pair had to wait some time before the screams died down.

"John Schaw, that is not what I ask." Sweat poured off Schaw's face, mixing with blood, a red trickle dripping down the rack's well-used boards. "You make this painful when it need not be. Why did you hide them from us?"

Schaw's bloodshot eyes flew open. "You take what belongs to every Scotsman to enrich yourself."

The questioner looked to his companion, who reached for the rack's oversized wheel, only stopping when he raised a hand. *Not yet.* A few more turns would snap tendon and bone. Men tended to faint when that happened, and unconscious men couldn't answer questions.

Questions such as where they'd hidden certain items.

"Our plan did not involve you," he said. "Tell me, Mr. Schaw. Tell me how you knew."

Schaw made a noise that could have been a laugh. "Your incompetent associate made mention of the scheme when I stood by."

As he'd suspected. "So, you decided to move them to keep everything from us."

"You will never have them," Schaw said.

The other tormentor, who had yet to speak, reached into his trouser pocket. Before the questioner could stop him, the man's fist slammed into Schaw's side. "Stop – you will kill him."

His companion shrugged and slipped the small blade back into his pocket. A new trickle of blood from Schaw's ribcage dripped onto the straw-covered floor, black in the torchlight.

"Tell me where they are," the questioner demanded. "Freedom will be your reward." Schaw spat at him.

"We tracked you through Scotland," the questioning man said. "You evaded us at first, but your time is at an end. Unless you tell us where they are hidden, you will die here."

"Then their location dies with me."

Schaw smiled. The peaceful grin of a man who knew his time had come and had no quarrels with it. John Schaw had done it not for money or for glory. He'd done it for love of country. A love so strong not even the threat of death could force him to betray his cause.

The questioner spoke to his companion. "Again." The wheel turned, cartilage tore, and John Schaw's cries bounced off the stone walls. "Tell me," the man said again, to no avail. Without prompting his associate tightened the wheel and a bone snapped.

"Where is it?" Shouting now, the questioner leaned in, grabbing Schaw's arm and twisting it until the shoulder popped with a sickening *crack*. "Tell me!"

Nothing but groans as the wheel turned again.

"Stop." They rotated the wheel in reverse, loosening the ropes now tearing John Schaw in half. "No. You do not die." Wood creaked as the ropes slackened, though John Schaw never moved.

Leaning over Schaw's mouth, the questioner waited for a hint of breath to warm his cheek. *You cannot die.* No breath came from the broken body.

John Schaw was dead. His secret, lost forever.

Chapter 1

Present Day
Edinburgh, Scotland

A man's elbows found the bar in one of Edinburgh's more anonymous pubs. A pint settled in front of him before the bartender returned to polishing glasses. His hand wrapped around the glass, and when it settled back atop the bar it was half-empty. A mirror ran behind the bar, bottles lining the lower half like sentinels along a castle wall. Not once did the mirror reflect this man's eyes, which remained on the drink he held as the foam settled.

A blanket of gray covered the sky. Church bells pealed nearby, heralding the noon hour with their heavy tones. The citizens of Edinburgh filled the sidewalks, furled umbrellas in hand with the promise of rain hanging over the streets. Storefronts of butchers, haberdasheries, bakers and pubs watched over Edinburgh's populace, some of them dating from before Scotland became part of Great Britain. Each, like every man and woman on the street, had a story to tell.

Some stories came easier than others. The drinking man inside the bar did not offer his, and the bartender didn't ask. This man raised his empty glass, and the bartender delivered a replacement.

"Any food today?" The man's head shook. "Right, then." The bartender went back to polishing glasses while a football match played on a dingy television overhead. This too escaped the drinking man's attention. Few people ventured into the quiet Edinburgh pub this early in the day. Those who did kept to themselves, focused on the task at hand. The drinking man liked this. It was why he'd come here today, the same as he did most days. He rarely ate, but pints were plentiful, and the bartender never suggested he'd had enough. If he ever learned the bartender's name, he'd tell him he liked that.

The small lunch rush came and went, limited to a single man in paint-splattered overalls downing two pints with one eye on the clock, the other on the football match. When the working man hurried back out, he glanced at his fellow drinker and then at the floor, studying boots speckled with any number of colors. The drinking man didn't mind. He'd stopped shaving a few months ago. The patchy beard did little to inspire casual conversation, though if anyone looked past his unkempt hair, they'd notice clothes of fine quality, much like the shoes he never cleaned. This was a man who drank his lunch most days, but he did so by choice, not necessity.

The bartender ambled over as he drained pint number four. "Another?"

"Just one," he said. "I've an appointment today."

The bartender nodded and pulled another draft. The man polished it off and then paid in cash, leaving a sizable tip. Floorboards worn to a shine by generations of feet creaked as he walked out to find a day as gloomy as when he'd left it. The beer helped keep his feelings at bay most days, but today was different. If he could have avoided this meeting in good conscience, he would still be at the pub.

"May as well get it over with," he said to nobody before settling into his car. Even before a native Scot heard his American English, this vehicle told everyone its driver hailed from across the pond. His was the only Ford Mustang GT around, and people stared as he drove past, the super-charged, burbling engine an alien feature in their world. A grin tugged at his lips for the first time that day.

His car maneuvered easily through the narrow city streets, bringing him to the University of Edinburgh. Part castle and part modern architecture, the ancient campus buildings seemed to brood over their newer brethren, though the building he parked near was all rough stone and dark mortar. Pain shot up one leg as he walked in, same as it always did after sitting too long. His doctor told him the skin graft needed time to heal and this would pass. If time could hurry up and get him fixed, he'd appreciate it.

He located the correct office door after a few false turns.

"Good morning, sir." An attendant greeted him with more perk than necessary.

"I have an appointment," he said.

Miss Perky glanced at the passport he offered and tapped her keyboard. "Yes, sir. The professor's class is nearly finished. If you'd like to wait here, she should be back any moment."

He pocketed his passport and took a seat. While the girl attacked her keyboard, thoughts he had tried to forget queued up and pushed for attention. No, he didn't want to be here. Not when all it could do was bring back what was better forgotten. He should leave. He didn't owe her anything, didn't have to do this.

A sigh escaped his lips. The only thing worse than facing this was pushing it back another day. He'd run out of excuses, believable or otherwise, and after six months in Scotland the idea of a familiar face other than the bartender's wasn't so bad.

Animated conversation from the hallway right outside the door made the decision for him. "Thank you, Professor." A man's voice carried to his ears. "I'll have those papers graded by Monday."

"No hurry," a woman said. "The undergraduate sections don't meet until mid-week, so take your time. Don't neglect your dissertation. I remember how many times I pushed mine back and ended up pulling all-nighters to catch up."

The man promised he wouldn't, and a few seconds later the professor walked in, her head buried in a textbook, scribbling as she walked.

"Your appointment is here," Miss Perky said.

"My appointment?" The professor looked up and noticed her visitor. "Oh, my." She stopped short. "You're here."

"I'm sorry it took so long." Parker Chase stood and offered a hand.

Chapter 2

July 7th
Edinburgh, Scotland

After shaking Professor White's hand, Parker reached up to smooth his unruly beard. *I should have at least trimmed this thing.*

"I completely understand," Jane said. "Please, come into my office."

Parker followed her into a cramped office dominated by a monstrous wooden desk and too many stacks of paper to count. He settled into an overstuffed leather chair and promptly banged his elbow on a coffeepot hidden behind a leaning pile.

"Sorry about the mess," Jane said. "Some jokester in administration thinks that because the history department deals with old things we should work in this ancient place." She leaned over him to grab the sliding stack before it toppled, and her brunette hair rustled past his nose. She tucked a lock behind one ear. "Care for a cup of coffee?"

The beer. Damn. "Coffee sounds great." What really sounded great was another pint.

While the machine bubbled and barked, Jane leaned on the edge of her desk, stood up, leaned back, and then finally sat on it, one foot off the ground. "Parker, I don't know what to say. I'm so sorry."

How many times had he heard that over the past seven months? How many times had he given the same meaningless platitude? *Thank you for your concern.* Enough to last a lifetime. His jaw tightened. Time for the truth.

"So am I," he said. "It still doesn't seem real."

Jane reached for his hand, then stopped, pulling hers back to tangle with the other in a grief-fueled knot. "I wish I could have come to the funeral."

"It was not a fun day." He'd sat in silence, facing an endless stream of mourners spanning Erika's past. Everybody had desperately wanted to be elsewhere. Not that he blamed them. Seeing his fiancée lying in a casket had made him want to run and hide. "I didn't realize how many friends she had."

"She was one of a kind." Jane leapt to her feet when the coffeemaker burbled to a finish. "Cream and sugar?" she asked, rushing to grab the pot.

"No thanks." Right now, the stronger the better. Hopefully strong enough to cover his boozy breath.

An engine roared to life outside Jane's open window before a riding lawnmower came past, the driver moving like a man who knew sunshine came at a premium around here and he intended to get the most out of it.

"What do you think of Edinburgh?" Jane asked once the mower zoomed past. "A bit quieter than Philadelphia."

"The history here is amazing." Erika may have been the history professor, but Parker loved the past more than most, part of why they'd clicked. "I haven't been outside the city as much as I'd like. What I have seen has been great." Spending so many hours in the pub limited his activities. "Getting out more is on my agenda before I leave."

"Are you leaving soon?" she asked. He shrugged. "No need to hurry. You've only been here, what, a month?"

"Going on six, actually."

She nodded, lips hidden behind the coffee mug. "Oh."

Parker sipped his coffee in silence. The mower outside came and went, a pair of students walked by on the sidewalk, and he still couldn't think of anything to say. Months without making small talk had really killed his social skills. Out of the ether, a thought struck. A snippet of bygone conversation. "Don't you have an interesting house?"

"You could say that," Jane said, smiling. "A bit different than what you get in the States." Her voice lightened. "Say, if you're around for a while yet, would you like to see it? It's just the caretaker and me these days, since my mother moved back to London and Dad headed off, but the place has plenty of charm."

"And interesting stories, I'd bet." Lifting his mug, Parker drank deeply, caffeine slicing through the alcohol fog. *Why not?* It wasn't like he had anything else to do. "It sounds great. Whenever is convenient for you."

She smacked his arm lightly. "Great," she said, the warmth in her words pulling him along for the ride. "How does tonight sound?" Parker said it was fine. "I can have Hugh tidy up, and if the rain holds, you'll be in for a treat. Our stained glass is top notch."

Jane's phone rang as the lawnmower made another pass. "Hello? Yes, this is she. Sure, bring it up." The handset clattered back down. "Is dinner time too late? I don't teach tonight, and if you can make it out by dinner, we'll have plenty of time to eat and give you the tour."

I really need to shave. He touched the unkempt beard. "Tonight is fine. Anything I can bring?"

"An appetite for learning. And for our food, of course. We have loads of local stuff in the pantry. You've never had cullen skink like my family makes it."

What in the world is cullen skink?

Jane's assistant appeared in her doorway. "Excuse me, Professor? There's a package for you."

"Bring it in, please."

The assistant didn't move. "Well, it's quite large. Heavy, too."

"I can grab it." Parker set his coffee on a paper pile, keeping a hand close until it stabilized.

He followed Jane through the door. "Goodness," she said. "You weren't kidding."

A metal box four feet long and nearly as high rested on a dolly. A delivery man slouched against the handle. "Sign here."

"Who is this from?" Jane asked, and she whistled softly when he told her. "They never said it was so *big*. Thanks for bringing it up."

"You were expecting this?" Parker asked.

"Yes," Jane said. She twisted her hair into a ponytail. "A colleague of mine in archeology is excavating part of Craigmillar Castle, which is only a few miles from here. During the dig they found an artifact and wanted me to examine it."

"Examine it in your office?"

"In the lab. If you don't mind grabbing my coffee, I'll wheel it down there." She grabbed the dolly, kicked the oversized box up and headed down the hall.

"I can take that," he said, scrambling to catch up.

"It's not far." She screeched around a corner and nearly flattened two young men. "One side, boys. Artifact coming through." Banging through a doorway, she led Parker into a well-lit room containing several glass tables. Cabinets covered both walls, displaying tools and gadgets he couldn't begin to identify.

"Help me lift this." Jane had already squatted down and grabbed hold. "On three." She counted, he hefted, and the metal box thudded onto a table.

"What is in there?"

"Human remains." She flipped the latches open. "Along with other materials, most likely clothing."

His eyes narrowed. "Wait, there's a body in there?" He peered into the box, where a black cloth covered the contents. "It doesn't weigh much at all."

"Corpses get lighter after a few hundred years." Jane pulled off the black sheet to reveal a stack of bones, definitely human. "My colleague found these remains behind a wall. She didn't have time to do a proper review, not with their schedule, so I offered to handle the exam." A flash drive appeared from a compartment inside the delivery box. "Photos of where they found the bones." Parker scrambled to catch the drive when she tossed it his way. "Pull the pictures up on that computer."

Too intrigued to do anything but follow orders, he connected the drive and found the first photo; a mounded pile of bones. "Your friend found everything in a big heap."

"That's interesting," she said. "The clothes survived remarkably well." Out came a plastic bag holding a dark material. Jane donned plastic gloves before laying the thick cloth on the table, then reached up and adjusted an overhead light so it fell on one specific area of what might have been a shirt in the eighteenth century. She pointed to a splotch on the dark blue cloth. "I'll bet you a dollar that's blood."

Parker squinted. "All of it? That's a big stain."

"It is, but blood makes sense," she said. "These bones were behind a partially collapsed wall. In the photos you can see the fallen bricks." Parker looked, and she was right. "People don't just crawl behind a wall and die."

"You think someone hid the body."

Jane did. "My colleague noticed that part of the wall because the mortar looked different. As though it had been patched up after the initial walls were built. If you want to hide a body, behind a wall of an abandoned castle is a good place."

"How old do you think this guy is?"

Jane's hands went on her hips. "Judging from the clothing, the history of the castle and what I know about this area, my guess is he died sometime around 1700."

Parker looked up. "What do you know about this area? That's a very specific guess based on a shirt."

"I have you at a disadvantage," she said, grinning. "Craigmillar Castle is well known. It was abandoned just before 1700 and hasn't been occupied since. It would have been a good location to bury this body." Jane indicated the digital images. "Break down a wall, toss this body in there, patch it up and be on your way."

"If that is a blood stain. it's all under one sleeve."

Jane shrugged. "Possibly a stab wound. If his ribs are in here, we may find a scrape or gouge."

While Jane unloaded the bones, laying them out in an approximation of a person lying down, Parker scanned the photos. "You can tell this is a man?"

"Yes. A male pelvis is more angled, while a female's is more rounded and wider for giving birth."

The jumble morphed into a nearly complete set of bones, stretching across the table. Then out of nowhere she said, "Look at this."

He frowned. "Looks like a wrist bone to me, but I'm not very good with anatomy."

"Not the bones. *This.*"

Some kind of fuzzy brown string. "What is it?"

"Rope strands," she said. "On both wrists."

"Okay."

"Look at his ankles."

Parker looked down and found more brown fiber that could have been rope. Or dried grass. Or fabric threads from a shirt. "Looks like more rope. Maybe."

She stepped toward him, holding the wrist bones. "Rope around the wrists and ankles," she said. "What does that suggest?"

The fog in his head cleared. "You think this guy was tied up." He looked around at the age-darkened castle walls, everything below ground. It screamed one thing. "This is a dungeon. This guy may have been tortured."

"Yes." The bones went back in place, and now she pointed to the trousers. "See these rips at the bottom? I'd bet ropes did that."

An image from the history books popped into Parker's mind. "This guy was on a rack?"

"That's what I'm thinking," she said.

"What about the blood stain?" Parker asked. "A rack wouldn't rip your side open, would it?"

"Not likely." Jane repositioned the shirt, and then squinted. "I didn't notice this before." She poked her finger through a hole smack in the stain's center. "This may be a puncture wound."

"You think this guy," Parker waved a hand over the assembled skeleton, "was stretched on a rack, and then someone stabbed him in the side? I thought the rack was used to make people talk."

Jane shrugged. "The evidence suggests that torture and death by stabbing are one possibility."

Parker snapped rubber gloves on. "Can I touch the shirt?"

"Yes," Jane said as she continued assembling the skeleton. "Don't rip anything if you can help it."

Nerves tingled in his gut, the kind he used to get helping Erika with her research. Nights he hadn't valued enough, hadn't appreciated for what they were. He took a deep breath.

As he turned the rough cloth strands over in his hands, Jane spoke. "You've been able to spend considerable time here in Edinburgh."

"I have my own company and good employees. They handle things while I'm away."

"That's great," she said. "What kind of business?"

"Investment banking. I was fortunate with my early investments, then hired the right people. Lets me oversee things from anywhere." Vague enough, but truthful. He didn't mention the bulk of his money had come from a dead man, but given the man had been trying to kill him at the time, it seemed like a fair trade.

"Working with a close-knit team is the best," she said. "My department is on the smaller side, so everyone gets to know each other."

The coarse fabric was heavier than modern clothes, built to endure heavy wear. At a time when most people had owned only a few articles of clothing, sturdiness was a virtue in shirts and trousers. A patch covered one elbow, darker and thicker than the rest. Parker rubbed the repair job. *Much thicker.*

"Jane, look at this." She glanced up. "This patch is odd. It's almost out of place."

"An elbow patch isn't unusual," she said. "Lots of stretching and moving going on there. It was easier to patch a shirt back then than buy a new one. Only wealthy people splurged on new clothes."

"It's not just the patch. Come here." Parker guided her hand. "Do you feel that? Almost as though—"

"– there's something *in there.*" Jane grabbed the shirt. "You're right." She held the sleeve to her ear and twisted. "It's definitely different." She pushed him aside and rummaged through a drawer. "Hold this."

A flashlight came his way, and with Parker providing the light, Jane moved the patch back and forth. "Anything?" Parker asked.

"Not yet. There's a scalpel in that cabinet." She pointed across the room. "Please get it for me." He followed her direction, and Jane took the gleaming steel blade and set the shirt down. "Stay out of the light."

Parker leaned back as she went to work. Jane plucked one stitch at a time until an entire side stuck up like a mad scientist's hair. "Normally I wouldn't do this," here she gave him a wink, "but I want to know what's in here."

"Fine by me."

Jane slipped her fingers through the opening she'd cut. They came back out holding a thick piece of paper, translucent under the lights. "My goodness."

"Is there writing on it?"

She ignored him. "It's in great shape. The wall blocked any light sources, and the temperature was consistent. Almost perfect preservation conditions." Jane laid the folded parchment on the table. "This isn't paper. It's vellum."

"Calf skin," Parker said. Jane looked up, raised an eyebrow. "I've seen it before," he told her.

"Then you know this was much more expensive than paper. If this man," she nodded to the bones, "wanted to write a message that wouldn't fade away or fall apart, vellum was a good choice."

"Are you going to open that, or do I have to do it for you?"

"Patience," she said. "Move the shirt for me."

He did. Jane grabbed a nearby camera, which clicked and flashed from every angle. "Now we can open it." She turned toward him. "Care to do the honors?"

He didn't give her a chance to change her mind. "Easy does it," she warned as the vellum unfolded into a square sheet roughly half the size of a modern piece of paper.

Dark letters filled the page.

"Bloody hell," she said. "It's a letter."

"It doesn't make sense to hide a blank piece of paper," Parker said.

"True, but you spend enough time with Erika to know research isn't like the movies. *X* doesn't usually mark the spot."

She had used the present tense. *Spend,* not *spent.* A small difference, but if the knife cut in the right spot, size didn't matter. "She taught me a thing or two. Can you read it?"

The cramped letters ran on top of each other, competing for space from end to end. Flourishes decorated the end of nearly every sentence. "Give me a minute," Jane said.

She fell silent, and Parker let her read. Another lesson from Erika.

"It's a story," she finally said.

"About what?"

"Why this man was murdered."

Chapter 3

July 7th
Edinburgh, Scotland

Parker stopped mid-blink. "Tell me the story."

"You should read this for yourself." She set the paper down. "Another pair of eyes is a good idea."

Parker smoothed out the heavy material, the crowded words pulling him back through the centuries as a strange tale unfolded.

My friend Philip,

I hear hooves pounding and feel the chill of steel drawing ever nearer, for those who pursue me gain ground by the day. I have taken a wandering course through our land, a ruse to evade those who would take our honours. If we see each other soon, then you will know success is ours.

My journey began after our routine assignment in Edinburgh. I have visited parts of our land, leaving a marker for you at each. Should I fail to escape, you must use these markers to find what is hidden. I dare not reveal the location here for fear that this missive might fall into their hands. However, Philip, you will see my footsteps. Follow them and retrieve what belongs to no man.

Look to the blood which brought victory over Longshanks' deposed heir. It is the soul from which Scotland springs, a source of inspiration beating for us all – and where to find the brightness you seek.

Your fellow patriot,

James

Parker looked up to find Jane watching him.

"Who are Philip and James?" he asked. Not much of the letter made sense, so he figured he might as well start there. "Should I know them?"

Jane tapped her fingers on the tabletop. "So far nothing comes to mind. Both were common names in the seventeenth century. Unless we find another clue to James's identity in the rest of these artifacts, the names aren't much help."

"It looks like whoever was chasing James found him," Parker said. "Was this the only skeleton at the site?"

"As far as I know. I'll call my colleagues now and make sure."

"It could be that Philip is there too," Parker said. "A second body would give us more clues."

"*Us?*" Jane winked. "Are you joining the team?"

The spark that had ignited when he read James's letter faded. No, he wasn't on her team. He wasn't on anybody's team. "No. This isn't my field."

Jane touched his arm. "I'd love to have you help with this. It's not every day you find a centuries-old map to follow."

His chin lifted. "You're going to follow this?"

"Of course I am," she said.

His back straightened, and the sunlight got a little brighter. "So where should we start?"

Footsteps sounded before Jane responded, and an unfamiliar voice called out from the hallway. "Hello? Dr. White?" Parker turned to find a man walking through the door. "There you are."

Jane smiled at the man. "Hi, Tom. What can I do for you?"

"How are the new artifacts?" The newcomer removed his glasses, rubbing them with the edge of an untucked polo. "I don't believe we've met," he said, extending a hand Parker's way. "Tom Gregan."

"Parker Chase." Tom had smooth skin; his grip was light.

"Forgive me," Jane said. "Parker is a friend of mine from America." Her voice faltered. "I used to know his fiancée."

Tom glanced back to Jane. "I see. It is nice to meet you, Mr. Chase. I hope you've found our university as appealing as we do."

"Call me Parker. It's interesting." He nodded to the stone walls. "We don't have places like this back home."

"A bit drafty, but they work for our purposes. Speaking of which," he turned back to Jane, "it seems you found the dead man."

"Tom is one of our administrators," Jane said. "He keeps track of everything we do. Mustn't waste any funding, you know."

"Grant money does not come easily," Tom said. "It's not all numbers, though. I enjoy learning a bit from you experts, even if most of it goes over my head."

"I understand," Parker said. "Jane, I'll get out of your way. Thanks for letting me stop by."

"Hold on." She handed him a card. "Call me later. You'll want to hear about our findings, I'm sure."

Her card hovered in the air. Jane took a step toward him, and then Parker reached out. "Of course," he said. "Talk to you soon." She nodded, and Parker looked to Tom Gregan. "Nice to meet you, Tom."

Tom didn't look up from the bones. "You as well."

Cool air slipped under his shirt as Parker navigated the drafty halls. While the spark of interest in his chest hadn't died, it didn't flare up either. It burned softly in a place where no light had been for six months, the place where he used to feel so alive. It wasn't the same, but nothing ever would be. He pushed the door open and took in the blue sky, letting the sun warm his face.

Chapter 4

July 7th

White smoke floated toward a mahogany ceiling. A glowing ember burned brightly as the woman inhaled and tobacco crackled. She reached toward a cut-glass ashtray and flicked her cigarette holder, sending ash fluttering in every direction. The day's last sunlight warmed one of her elbows, currently propped on a stone window ledge.

A telephone rang. As she smoked, the noise stopped, replaced by footsteps. Moments later a door opened and her butler's voice called out.

"Miss? You have a call."

"Who is it?"

"He would not say, Miss. Only that it is urgent."

Her cigarette holder clattered into the ashtray. "Put him through." Heels clicked as she walked to her desk and waited for the phone to light up. When it did, she flicked a stray strand of silver hair away and answered. "Who is this?"

"I have something which may interest you."

Him. Her stomach tightened. "Is that so?"

"This may be the most intriguing one to date."

She gripped the phone tighter as the man spoke. "I assume you require funding. More money."

"Yes." The man coughed. "Have I ever let you down before?"

He had not. All one had to do was look around this very room to see the fruits of his labors. "You wouldn't be working any longer if you did. What do you need?" As she listened, a golden cross on the wall glinted in the fading sunlight. One of her caller's better finds, taken from an Irish monastery. A world-class example of Middle Age craftsmanship. Art a woman like her appreciated. Beautiful, but not even the room's nicest piece, let alone the best of the many on display across her residence's thirty-eight rooms.

"Do you approve?" he asked after the silence had stretched on.

"The money will be there tomorrow," she said. "I expect updates as you go. Anything you find comes first to me."

"Of course. I will be in touch."

Her high heels clicked as she returned to the windowsill to find her cigarette dead. A new one appeared, an ivory lighter flared and hot smoke filled her lungs. *What could it be?* He always delivered, and nothing but the best. For that, she paid handsomely.

She turned back to the desk, skirt twirling as she buzzed the butler's line. "A cocktail. Gin martini, two olives." A tingle rose through her body, and she smiled. A new piece in her collection. *How delightful.*

Chapter 5

July 7th
Barnbougle Castle

Parker let out a whistle when he pulled up to Jane's house. As if you could call it a house. Looming over him, blocking out what little daylight remained, Barnbougle Castle had jumped from the past and landed smack in Parker's way as he motored down the heavily wooded driveway.

Erika had mentioned that Jane's family had an ancestral home that defied description, with some link to lower nobility Parker had heard and forgotten in the same breath. At the time, other matters had been weighing on his mind. He sighed. Damned if he could remember what had mattered more than listening to her.

A spotlight lit the grounds as Jane stepped out the front door and waved. Parker passed a low-slung wall surrounding the structure on three sides. The castle was shaped like a rectangle, nearly as tall as it was long, the highest points of an expansive roof looking down on Parker from over forty feet above. At the back of the property the castle overlooked a vast body of water stretching nearly to the horizon, the far-distant shore showing the outline of downtown Edinburgh.

"Good evening," she said. "Thank you for coming."

"Quite the place you have here." He looked up at the stone walls stretching toward the sky, the crenellated roof with lookout posts and towering chimneys. "I wouldn't want to try a frontal assault."

Jane laughed. "Personally, I would row across the lake at night. Surprise attacks work best." She wrapped her arms around her torso, shivering in the wind. "Come in. Even in summer we get a breeze off the lake."

A small plaque beside the front door read *Barnbougle circa 1201*. Talk about history. Following Jane through an aged wooden door now solid as stone, he found a wide staircase leading to the second story and other parts unknown. Doors twice his height branched off on two sides, each open and throwing patches of light on the marble floors. "Welcome to Barnbougle Castle," Jane said. "Or as I like to call it, my cozy flat."

"You could house a small army here," he said. "How many rooms are there? I bet you get lost in here at times."

Jane laughed. "It's laid out like a grid, hallways going north to south or east to west. Three floors, though most of the second floor has double-height ceilings, which makes it seem larger. Once you walk around for a few minutes you can find your way. And I'm not certain about the number of rooms. There must be dozens. We only use a handful of them. What's the use of having so much space for only two?"

"You have a roommate?"

"Of a sort. Come on, I'll introduce you." She led him deeper inside, and he paused to stare at the library. "You have an actual library," he said. "There must be thousands of books in here." Volumes stretched toward the ceiling, two stories overhead.

"I've read most of them," she said. "You can borrow anything you like." He followed Jane as they passed beneath an archway, headed toward the crackle of burning wood. A rich, earthy aroma grew until Parker found a roaring fire, the flames reaching well past his waist. A man crouched in front of the grate, poking the logs. "Hugh, our guest is here."

The tall man turned around to present one of the finest beards Parker had ever seen. Thick, curly, and white as snow, it tumbled in a waterfall from the closely cropped silver hair atop his head. "Good evening, young sir. Hugh Burton, at your service." He offered a hand.

The old guy had a grip like iron. "Parker Chase. Nice to meet you."

"Hugh is as much a part of this place as the stones and mortar," Jane said. "I don't ever remember him not being here."

Embers glowed as Hugh puffed on his pipe. "And I remember the first time you came through the front door. The tiniest little lass. Bawling like a banshee, this one was. Never heard a babe scream so loud." Wrinkles formed at the corners of Hugh's eyes. "What a beautiful sound."

"You need a new story," Jane said.

Hugh laughed softly. "Very true, my dear, but I try to remember the good times." Now the wrinkles disappeared, along with his grin. "Things have changed here."

Jane skipped over and grabbed one of his arms. "You and I are still here. What more do we need?"

Hugh studied the floor. "True." He looked up to Parker. "Visitors are welcome here. I hope you find Barnbougle to your liking, Mr. Chase. There is plenty to do on these grounds."

"Call me Parker." He waved a hand toward the front door. "I imagine there's good hunting in those woodlands."

"Do you hunt?" Hugh asked.

"All my life. Are you familiar with Pennsylvania?" Hugh nodded without conviction. "We have plenty of woods for hunting deer, turkey, all types of game."

"This estate offers more than enough to keep us fed, but since Jane's father left, nobody has shot in these woods but me." Hugh stepped back to the fire. "Lord White's firearm is here waiting for him." Hugh pointed to a rifle hanging above the mantel. "I clean it, keep it ready for action."

"Is he away on business?" Parker asked.

Hugh's eyes flitted to Jane. "A contentious divorce," she said. "He and my mother decided time away from Edinburgh was best. My father is in England, 'recapturing his youth'." She frowned. "Hiding from the problem is my opinion, but he won't listen. Mother is doing the same in France. Hugh and I have the place to ourselves for the foreseeable future." The old man grinned. "There are worse places to be. But you didn't come to hear about my parents. We have a mystery to unravel." She grabbed his hand. "Everything is in my office."

She half-dragged him around a corner to an office several halls away. A low fire burned inside, the stone and mortar motif the same as in every room he'd seen, with dark corners and tall windows. Jane used a poker to jab the wood. "It's all there." She pointed to a desk roughly the size of a sailboat. "Tom and Evan reviewed your find. You created quite a stir."

"Evan?" Parker asked as he looked at the stacks of paperwork. *Where is that letter?*

"My graduate assistant. He's been working with me for several years now." A sap pocket burst in the fire. "Exceptional student, but he can't decide on a dissertation. He'd have graduated two years ago if he didn't keep changing topics. Tough for his pocketbook, but good for me."

Parker shuffled through the documents. "Did you learn anything else about the letter or the corpse?" *Ah, here it is.* A copy of the original letter sat atop a pile, along with photos of the letter from multiple angles. "If we figure out who Philip and James are, we'll have more luck understanding what this means."

Jane walked over. "Identifying two men from hundreds of years ago based on their first names won't be easy. Both names were even more common then than they are today."

"Does anyone jump out at you, maybe royalty or military?"

"Well, James I was the first king of both Scotland and England, and he lived close to the right time period. Before he was James I, he was known as James VI of Scotland. The same for Philip. There was a King Philip of Spain, England and Ireland, and that's just one of the Philips. Spain had many of them."

Parker frowned. "And if we get into non-royalty, it will be even worse."

"We use the other clues. Like this." Jane tapped the photocopied letter. "Our James started the assignment in Edinburgh. What assignment, we have no idea, but let's assume since he's in Edinburgh, James was Scottish. It's a common Scottish name, and people then weren't as mobile, so if James was in Edinburgh when he wrote this letter, there's a good chance he was born or spent time in Scotland."

Parker read the letter again. "Okay, but it doesn't get us any closer to figuring out who they were."

Jane walked away and flipped the lights on. A window overlooking the lake framed millions of glittering dots on the water beneath a blazing half-moon. "Then we take a different path if the name hunt isn't promising."

"I like this paragraph." He tapped the final sentences. "'*Look to the blood which brought victory over Longshanks' deposed heir.*' I helped Erika with her research, and cryptic statements like this usually turn out to say more than you'd believe." Research was an understatement, but now wasn't the time to get into that.

Jane winked. "You would have made a good historian."

"I have no idea what it means."

She laughed. "I'm Scottish. One word – *Longshanks*."

Parker cocked an eyebrow. "What's a Longshanks?"

"Not what. *Who*. Longshanks in all likelihood refers to King Edward I of England. A nickname about his height."

"Oh. *Long shanks*, as in long legs. I get it."

"He was six foot two. People weren't as tall in the thirteenth century." Her gaze ran the length of Parker's frame. "You're about his height. You'd have been considered huge in that time."

"So, is this the deposed heir?"

Jane pulled a sheet of paper from behind the photocopied letter. "This is a biography of Longshanks' son, Edward II. He ruled England after his father died in 1307 until he was deposed in a coup twenty years later, and his son Edward III took the throne."

"Not very original in the name department."

"No, they weren't. Edward II carried on his father's campaign to suppress the Scottish rebellion. There is one specific battle history remembers more than the others. The Battle of Bannockburn in 1314. An outnumbered Scottish army defeated the English and turned the tide for the rebellion."

"Like our Battle of Gettysburg."

"Yes," Jane said. "It was a turning point that eventually led to Scottish independence, as Gettysburg led to the Confederacy's defeat."

"You think the letter references that battle?"

"It makes sense," Jane said. "Edward II lost, and you can trace a line from that failure to losing Scotland entirely. The letter refers to it as a *'victory'*. A clue we're dealing with a Scot. If he were any other nationality, the phrasing would differ."

That's promising. "Which leaves one part about this paragraph." He reached over and adjusted the desk lamp.

"It's getting late," Jane said. "Are you expected back home?"

"No, I left the dog door open for Tory. He can let himself out."

"I didn't know you have a pet."

"I got him a few months ago," Parker said. "I happened to walk by the shelter and figured I might as well meet the animals, take one for a walk. Tory caught my eye, so I took him out for a stroll, and you know how that can turn out. He's a big, lazy terrier mix. Probably sleeping now."

"That's wonderful," Jane said. Her hand moved toward his and then stopped. "Animals are the best. We always had dogs growing up, but our last one died a few years ago, and I haven't made time to get a new one."

"I'll bring Tory by some time if you'd like. He'd love to run around out here."

"Do that." Her eyes fell back to the desk. "There's one more part of this paragraph to study. *'Look to the blood which brought victory over Longshanks' deposed heir.'* What blood brought victory over Edward II? This part stumped me at first."

Parker's chest tingled like he'd taken a sudden breath of cool air. "At first? Is it a metaphor?"

"For what, though? Blood can indicate love, hate, loyalty, death or any other number of ideas. We were stuck until Evan had a thought. What if it's not symbolic at all, but real? Something associated with physical blood."

Parker frowned. "You mean like a bloody weapon? Sometimes they take on a life of their own. Excalibur, for instance."

"Close, but not what we came up with." She leaned closer. "We got to the *heart* of the matter."

"Tell me what an actual heart has to do with a three-century-old letter found in a dead guy's shirt."

Instead of answering, Jane leaned over the keyboard on her desk. "This last part tells us Philip and James are Scottish. Remember, James has been to multiple locations and left markers to help Philip find *'what belongs to no man'*," she said. "Assuming James stayed in Scotland, we can focus on how this makes sense through a Scottish lens. Here's one way." A partially ruined building came up on her monitor, curved archways with no roof fronted by manicured lawns, columns rising in the background. "That's Melrose Abbey. It's been around since the fourteenth century. Today it's part ruins, part museum."

"You think Melrose Abbey may tie in with the blood reference?"

The fire sent orange light dancing across her face. "Robert the Bruce, King of Scots, defeated Edward II at the Battle of Bannockburn. When Robert died years later, his body was buried at Dunfermline Abbey. However, before that, one of his chief lieutenants removed Robert's heart and stored it in a silver container which he wore around his neck to honor his king."

The cool tingle in Parker's chest spread to his arms and legs. A feeling he hadn't experienced in six months. "Is the heart still around?"

A knot burst in the fireplace, sending sparks everywhere. "It's buried at Melrose Abbey."

Chapter 6

July 8th
En route to Melrose, Scotland

Two tons of Detroit steel roared over the twisting two-lane road in Scotland's placid countryside, sheep and citizens alike turning as the screaming vehicle burst into their lives. Parker downshifted as they climbed a small rise and the seat pressed against his back, Jane beside him with both hands grabbing the seat. Despite this, he got the feeling she was enjoying the drive.

"Is your gear stowed tight?" Jane had insisted on loading the trunk herself when he'd picked her up this morning, what looked like an excavation tool set along with a duffel bag, contents unknown. Some people thought Scotland's rural roads required cautious handling. Parker knew they did, but that didn't mean driving like a geriatric. With all the speed Ford Motors had packed under this hood, leaving it untapped was criminal.

"It will be fine," she said. "And you didn't have to shave on my account."

Parker touched his smooth chin. "Half the year was long enough. Had to see if I remembered how to do it." His skin felt baby-soft after so long away from a razor, and was practically bleached. Maybe he'd get a haircut soon. For now, the rubber band from that morning's paper held it back, out of his face.

"I appreciate you driving," she said. "I'm sure you have other things on your calendar besides chauffeuring me around."

Considering his plans had been to post up at his usual bar stool and watch soccer all day, the promise of doing something worthwhile had lifted his spirits. "Tory will miss me, but I have a buddy coming by to feed him until I get back." That said buddy was the bartender at his watering hole remained a secret. Six months in Edinburgh and the only person he could call a "friend" was the guy who poured his drinks.

"I'll make it up to Tory when we get back," Jane said. "He can come over and run the grounds all he likes."

She held on tightly as they took a turn at speed. "I don't want to step on anybody's toes in joining this research," Parker said. "Are you sure your administrator and grad assistant don't mind?"

"Tom is more of an office guy, and Evan needs to work on his dissertation. You coming along is great. You're saving Tom from paying mileage out of the department budget. Anything that saves a pound is okay with him."

"Good to know. Did you learn anything else last night?"

"Records confirm Robert the Bruce's heart was buried separately from his body. Another of his military advisors took the heart with him on a campaign against the Moors, then brought it back to Scotland to be buried at Melrose Abbey. The heart has remained there for nearly seven hundred years."

"James the letter-writer would expect the heart to remain there forever."

"Yes," Jane said. "Now we have to figure out what James was saying he left behind."

Parker slowed as they rounded a bend and came headlight-to-tail with a pair of cows on the road. "Hold on." As he veered onto the grass, the one-ton behemoths didn't so much as moo when his door nearly scraped their haunches. "Do you think James would have left something that's still around today? The letter implies he didn't know when Philip would be coming."

"That's in our favor," Jane said. "My first thought was a message left with someone – perhaps one of the clergy or staff. My second idea was graffiti, like a message scratched into the stonework."

"It could be tough to identify now. There wasn't anything in the letter telling where to look."

Jane's shoulders dropped. "I know. Also, James could have told Philip where to find it. Say something he would recognize, a location or object with meaning only to them. We could be looking right past the answer now and never know it."

"Look on the bright side. James's message was never delivered, so if there's anything to find in the abbey it should still be there. If that's true, then we'll find it."

Her shoulders went back up. "You're right. If it's there, we'll find it." Jane put her palm out, and Parker slapped it. "Hit the gas, Mr. Chase."

Twenty minutes later Parker rolled to a stop in Melrose Abbey's parking lot, just across from the main attraction. "Looks like we're the first visitors today," he said. The lot was empty, though he'd passed several cars in Melrose's less-than-bustling downtown. A small village, really, with green fields and plots stretching in every direction. A stone wall stood guard along the abbey's front lawn. Oak and fir trees towered above the wall, and on the other side of an iron fence, rows of tombstones marked the abbey's graveyard, home to several Scottish kings and other nobles.

"Fewer people to notice us going places we shouldn't. Come on." She opened the door and the sweet scent of flowers filled the car. "Time to see what James was talking about."

Ages-old stone bathed in crisp morning light cast narrow shadows over the property. A lone car zipped by as they crossed the street, headed toward the cemetery. On the far side of the grounds a single brick building stood watch over neatly plowed fields and trees heavy with leaves.

"The ruins are over there," Jane said as they passed under the pointed front door. Half of a building's former exterior waited to one side, two walls joined at right angles nearly attached to the main building, as though a giant hand had descended from the heavens to lift the roof off. "Check inside for free literature. You never know what you'll find."

"I've never seen a downspout like that." Parker pointed to a sandstone pig that directed runoff from the roof. "Is he playing bagpipes?"

"He is," Jane said. "Very patriotic, that pig." Cool air brushed Parker's arms when they walked inside. An attendant waited at a small desk, head bowed over the morning paper. Jane cleared her throat. "Good day."

The paper rustled, and a tartan flat cap lifted. "Welcome to Melrose Abbey." Blue eyes twinkled in a face lined with a lifetime of experience. The man stood and offered his hand. "How may I help you?"

"We'd like to walk about and enjoy the grounds." Jane deposited several bills in the donations box. "It's such a lovely abbey, and the weather is perfect."

"That it is," the man said. "If there is anything I can do for you, please let me know."

"I do have one question." The elderly man leaned forward. "My friend and I are interested in Robert the Bruce. I understand part of the king's remains are here."

"The old Bruce's heart," he said. "A national treasure to us, my dear. Take one of those." He pointed to a stack of pamphlets. "It tells all about the Bruce's gift to our abbey. The site is through that door, right off the path."

Jane thanked him and grabbed a pamphlet, following Parker to the door. He opened it and sunlight warmed his face. "The heart is outside?"

"Halfway down the path," the man said. "Keep walking. You won't miss it."

Gravel crunched underfoot. "Why would they keep such a prized artifact outdoors? Doesn't seem safe."

"Not if it's underground," Jane said, her nose in the pamphlet. "It's buried like a body would be, with a marker on the spot." She looked up. "There it is."

Parker stopped in front of a concrete pipe jutting up from the ground. Letters ran across the top and bottom. Letters inscribed by a terrible speller. "What's it say?"

"It's a quote from a Scots poem," she said after consulting the pamphlet. "'*A noble hart may have nane ease gif freedom failye.*' The modern translation is 'A noble heart can know no ease without freedom.'"

"Mean anything to you?"

"Not really," Jane said. "It's from a poem written in 1375, so the significance escapes me. However, all is not lost." She pulled out her phone. "Give me a minute to check the university archives."

Parker strolled through the lines of gravestones while she attacked her phone. Time had weathered many of the headstones smooth, leaving only faint shadows of the inscriptions. With birds chirping in nearby trees and scarcely another soul in sight, Parker closed his eyes and an image popped into his head, the same one that returned every night. The blinking red light. A sharp flash of white. *Stop it.* Everything Scotland surrounded him, yet his thoughts turned to the explosion six months past that had changed his life.

He felt the rush of heat, the burning skin as fire singed his flesh. Pain lanced up his leg from the damn skin graft. Dryness crept up his throat. He needed a drink.

Jane called out, pulling him back to the present. "Look at this."

"Tell me you have good news."

"Nothing in the university database," she said. "There is plenty of information on Robert the Bruce's heart and the abbey, none of it helpful. However…" She slipped her phone into a pocket. "What did I tell you about local information?" She pulled the pamphlet out.

"You're kidding," Parker said.

Her eyes sparkled in the sunlight. "The abbey has worship areas in both the preserved and ruined sections. One of the ruined areas contained a baptismal fountain, and even though the building is partially gone, the fountain is still there. Guess what it's called?" She turned the pamphlet around so he could see. "The *Well of Souls.* Ring a bell?"

Parker snapped his fingers. "From the letter. What did it say? *'The soul from which Scotland springs.'* It makes sense. Did the fountain exist in James's time?"

"It dates from the sixteenth century. A hundred years before James wrote the letter."

A car rumbled into the parking lot across from them, diesel engine burbling. "Lead the way, Dr. White." Energy tingled through his legs, pushing the skin graft pain away. "Let's see what James left for us."

"Don't get ahead of yourself." A path led them under an arched doorway no longer supporting a roof, shadows flashing across the ground until Jane stopped in between three standing walls. The fourth had disappeared years ago.

"Look ahead." A stone pillar and bowl stood near one of the remaining walls, protected above by an archway and on either side by stacked stones. "It's almost entirely out of the elements," Jane said. "According to this, it was used for baptisms and other ceremonies."

"You check the walls. I'll take the fountain."

She grabbed his arm. "Hold on. You're not sticking me with boring walls. We check the fountain together." She tugged him back and darted toward the fountain. "I have no idea what to look for, so if you see anything strange, call it out."

He bent down, using his phone's flashlight to inspect the base. A solid block of gray stone flecked with dark specks supported the bowl. He ran his fingers over the stone; the edges were scarcely dulled despite centuries in the open. No cracks, no marks, nothing to grab his eye. "This base doesn't look promising."

"The bowl is in amazing shape," Jane said from above. "There's a dragon carved on the side. Strange, even for Scottish priests."

"Do you think it's possible James wanted Philip to look at the floor around this thing? It wouldn't be easy to leave a message on the fountain. Easier to pull out a stone and hide something underneath."

"I hope he didn't do that," Jane said. "Anything underneath any stones would have been waterlogged and rotted long ago. Besides, these stones are practically polished from all the rain."

Parker touched one of the mortared stones beneath their feet. She was right. Any markings on them had worn off years before. "I don't see anything," he said.

"The bowl's carvings are fantastic," Jane said. "And completely useless. They don't move, don't have any marks or notes, and I can't see anything out of the ordinary." She sighed heavily. "I'll check the walls."

When she trudged away, a weight descended on Parker's shoulders. *She won't find anything there.* Why he thought that, he couldn't say, other than just having lived through these past months. One after another, all the cards had landed against him, and he no longer had the energy to fight back. His hand tightened to a fist, and for an instant he wanted to punch the pillar, break the damn thing in half.

His fingers loosened. What was he thinking? He reached up to steady himself, and pain slashed across his knuckles. *What the hell?* The pillar wasn't smooth underneath that bowl. It was damned sharp. Blood trickled down his fingers.

What's there? He angled the phone's flashlight up and forgot about his knuckles. "Hey, Jane. Come look at this."

She ran over. "What?"

"Under the bowl." He aimed the light toward the base of it. "Look at the stone. Or *stones*."

She dropped to her knees. "The pillar isn't one solid piece. It's made from stone and mortar, just like the walls."

The pillar's top third was crafted not from a single stone, but from many put together. "Maybe the original pillar cracked and they repaired it."

"Or they wanted to raise the bowl and couldn't cut a new pillar." She pulled her phone out and flicked on the light. "Check the other side."

Parker did, and the breath caught in his throat. "I'll be damned."

Cut into a stone at the intersection of bowl and pillar, it had been hidden in the shadows. A jagged *P* carved into one stone. Parker rubbed the letter. No, he wasn't seeing things. "What do you think?"

"I think you found it!" Her words bounced off the walls, and Jane covered her mouth. "Or at least found a possible note from James." She cleared her throat. "Someone definitely carved this. It's not natural. Look, you can see along the edges where the tool slipped." She touched a wayward scratch. "My guess is a knife."

"James carved Philip's initial into this stone," Parker said, and Jane's mouth opened. "Wait." He raised a hand. "Go with me on this. We *assume*," and Jane nodded, "James carved this. Based on his letter, it makes sense. He directed Philip here, and this wasn't the last stop on his path. For Philip to get further along, he'd need more information. The *P* tells him he's on the right track, though it doesn't tell him where to go next."

"Agreed," Jane said. "So, the question is, how does Philip know what to do now?"

Parker reached into his pocket and produced a Leatherman utility knife, the same kind he had carried since he started hunting as a boy. "This pillar is in great shape considering how old it is. Still, it's been outside for a long time and whatever's holding it together isn't as strong as it used to be. See?" A chunk of gray mortar broke loose when he scraped it. "If I'm James and I want to leave information for Philip, how do I do it?"

He took another gouge out of the mortar.

"You think he removed this stone," Jane said. "And what, left a message behind it?"

"Or something to point Philip on the right track," Parker said. A quick check confirmed they were alone. "We were looking for something like this scratched letter and we nearly missed it. Unless you expected to find something, who would see it? All James had to do was come into the church when no one was around and leave this marker for Philip."

"He could have done this quickly," Jane said.

Dust and grit crumbled under Parker's knife. With Jane keeping watch, he hacked around the stone, searching for leverage. He paused when an elderly couple strolled past, standing protectively around the baptismal bowl until they moved along. With renewed vigor he went back at it, sweat beading on his forehead as he attacked the stone.

"I think I can get it," he said. The blade caught, bending as he tried to lever the stone out. "Do you have anything stronger than my knife? It's going to break."

"Hold on." Jane ran to her car and returned with a small handbag. "We use these tools for cleaning artifacts," she said. A metal file came out, long and slender with rough patterns on each side. "That stone should break before this does."

"I knew I brought you for a reason," Parker said. He took a breath. "Here goes nothing."

He jammed the file behind the stone, levering gently at first, then harder when nothing happened. "Stand back." With Jane out of harm's way, he leaned back, the metal file biting into his palm. Mortar crackled and the blade stuck, until all at once it let go and Parker ended up on his backside, the stone in his lap. Or rather, half the stone. As he'd tumbled, a brown object had fallen to the ground.

Jane scooped it up. "It's leather," she said. "A thin sheet rolled and tied together."

"This stone is hollow." He held it up. "Look, you can see scrape marks." Parker jumped up and showed her the rough scratches inside the hollowed-out interior. "A knife could have made them."

"The same knife used to carve Phillip's initial," Jane said. "So he could hide this."

The dark leather sheet crackled as Jane twisted it and several flakes floated to the ground. An image flashed across Parker's mind. "Erika always wore gloves when she found artifacts." He said it without thinking. His throat went dry.

"Any oil from my fingers won't hurt it," Jane said. She paused and looked closely at his face. "There's a message here. I can see—"

Parker dropped the stone and grabbed Jane's shoulder, turning her away from the approaching footsteps as he kicked the broken stone against the pillar. "Hide it."

She was still fumbling with it when a voice called out behind them. "Hello, friends."

Parker shielded Jane from view, turning to find the white hair and broad smile of the front desk attendant. "Hello," he said. Jane muttered, elbowed his back.

"A lovely day for your visit," the man said. "Are you enjoying our abbey?"

"We are. It's amazing how these ruins have held up over time."

"That it is," he said. "And you, young lady. How do you find the grounds?"

Jane bumped into Parker, knocking him off balance and away from her. "Lovely," she said. "We were just admiring this baptismal font."

"A fine piece of craftsmanship." The man walked toward them. The broken stone was in plain view if he looked at the ground. "Thousands were brought into the house of our Lord with that bowl," he said. Parker stepped back, trying to hide it.

"I can imagine," Jane said as she stepped toward the attendant. "We're lucky to have the place nearly to ourselves. I'm sure it's normally more crowded."

"Now most travelers want to visit the city, see castles and landmarks. Religion and small abbeys don't interest them. I suspect

Robert the Bruce's heart keeps us alive as much as anything. Ironic, yes?" They let him chat on. What would the old guy say if he knew the abbey's history wasn't just alive, but was changing as he spoke?

"This place is wonderful," Parker said when the man stopped for a breath. "We'll be sure to stop by your desk if we have any questions."

The attendant nodded and walked off.

"What were you thinking?" Parker asked once the footsteps faded. "Admiring the baptismal bowl, calling his attention to it."

"I couldn't think of anything else to say." Jane reached into her shirt. "Let's see what this says."

Lines creased Parker's forehead. "Where did you hide that?"

"The last place a kind old man would look. Stop staring." Parker's cheeks grew hot as she unfolded the leather. "I was right," she said. Jane cleared her throat and began reading.

Philip,

I carry the weight of our nation with me. Those who would profit from our loss are close behind. My route will lead to where my namesake gained his first crown. Look to our compatriot I. A.

James

Birds chirped as the breeze returned, and a car motored past the church. Parker grabbed the half-stone and shoved it back into the pillar before anyone else happened by. "Does that mean anything to you?"

"It means we're on the right path." Still holding the letter, she wrapped her arms around him, dancing a crazy jig that sent gravel flying. "Can you believe it?"

He hadn't been this close to a woman in six months. "Pretty neat," he said before pulling free. "What won't be neat is if you destroy the letter."

"Good point." She re-folded the message and slipped it into her pocket. "I've never done anything like this before."

"You mean made history instead of study it?"

"That's *exactly* what I mean. And we're just getting started."

Parker cocked an eyebrow. "How's that?"

"James is giving Philip directions, and I know where they lead." She tapped her pocket. "James mentions his 'namesake'. He says it's where this other James 'gained his first crown'."

"So we're talking about *King* James," Parker said. "You know who King James is?"

"There were a few. At least six I know of. James and Philip were Scottish, so we can focus on Scottish, Irish and English royalty."

"There are still a half-dozen kings to sort through."

Jane disagreed. "Not quite. It mentions 'his first crown'. This means James was either king at two different times, or he ruled over two nations. My money is on the latter."

"You have a reason for this."

"Only one James was king of two different countries and gained those crowns *at different times*." She clapped rapid-fire, hands tight in front of her chest. "King James VI of Scotland ruled his native country for decades before Elizabeth I died childless in 1603. When she did, he became King James I of England."

"What about that 'weight of our nation' stuff?" Parker asked.

Jane shrugged. "No clue. And I have no idea who their compatriot is either. It's hard to tell when you only have initials, assuming that's what they are."

Soft footsteps again crunched over gravel, growing louder as voices reached Parker's ears. "Let's get out of here. Even that nice old guy won't believe anyone is this interested in a baptismal bowl."

Parker started back toward the main abbey, only to turn and find Jane headed the other way. "Where are you going?"

"Straight to the car," she said. "We have to get moving."

"Moving?" he asked, jogging to catch her. "Where?"

"To where King James VI gained his first crown." They passed one of the few other cars in the parking lot, the driver's nose buried in an oversized map. "I know where it happened."

Parker grabbed his phone. "Do we need a flight to London? I have a ton of miles we could use—"

Jane cut him off. "Not London." She popped the rear hatch and tossed her tool bag inside. "We're driving, not flying." The rear hatch slammed shut. "He was crowned in one of Scotland's most famous churches. The Church of the Holy Rude. It's ninety minutes from here."

"Then strap in." The Mustang's engine roared when Parker turned the key. He didn't want that drink any longer. Maybe to celebrate, but first, they had a church to see. His tires found the road and the car jumped, throwing them back into the seats as the abbey receded in his mirrors.

In the parking lot behind them, a man lowered the map he had been reading and twisted a key in the ignition. The engine came to life, and he drove out of the parking lot with a phone pressed to his ear. "Yes, I have them. No, they didn't have anything with them. I'll be in contact." He clicked off and sent gravel flying as he cut off an oncoming delivery truck, racing to catch up to the American sports car.

Chapter 7

July 8th
Church of the Holy Rude
Stirling, Scotland

Even in the afternoon sun, Holy Rude brooded over the town. The church's tower stood watch, every stone and wall a defense tested time and again over the centuries. He and Jane might have been on the trail of an ages-old mystery hidden for hundreds of years, but to this church it was nothing more than a minor diversion.

"Impressive, isn't it?" Jane studied the tower as Parker rumbled over a stone bridge he hoped wouldn't choose now to collapse. "It was founded in 1129, but the original structure burned down. This version dates from 1405."

"It was a hundred years old when Christopher Columbus sailed to America."

"Makes you feel young, doesn't it?" Jane leaned back, stretching her arms over her head. "Unfortunately, lots of history means lots of possible answers to our question."

"Who," Parker said, "or what, is *I.A.*, and why James told Philip to look there."

Winding through town, they passed restaurants, busy produce stands with nearly empty shelves, and more than a few dark pub doors. Parker lowered his window at a stoplight. "That smells delicious." The scent of deep-fried chickpeas came from a nearby food truck. "I'm starving. You want some falafel?"

Jane did, and after downing two orders they continued on to Holy Rude, driving through the shade of its thick oak trees alongside an expansive graveyard. He found a parking spot outside the front entrance. "Bigger crowd here than at Melrose Abbey," he said. "I hope we don't have to damage any more Scottish history."

"I like to think we recovered it." Jane left her tools in the car this time and they headed for the front door. "Nothing in our archives references a person with those initials, so off the top of my head I can't tell you what they mean."

Parker took in the weathered stones and brilliant stained-glass windows, alive with sunlight. "Do you know anyone who has studied this church? From what you said it's an important place."

Jane shook her hair out and then tied it back behind her head. "I'm copying your style."

Heat bloomed on his cheeks. "I know. I need a haircut." Parker touched his locks. *Maybe she doesn't see how dingy the rubber band is.*

She winked. "I'm kidding. It looks nice. The monarchy has been associated with Holy Rude for centuries. James VI was crowned here, although I don't know any experts on this place. If this were Stirling Castle, we could talk to my grad assistant Evan. His dissertation involves the castle."

"Is that Stirling over there?" Parker pointed to a sprawling estate set atop the highest hill around, all dark stone and sharp points.

Jane said it was. "Cliffs on three sides and a perfect covering view of the River Forth. If you want to take that castle, you'd better be willing to sacrifice an army."

They ducked into Holy Rude's cool interior and walked across a rainbow. Parker looked up. "Now that's impressive. Getting a window that size so high without modern technology." The stained-glass window, depicting biblical scenes, stretched nearly to the ceiling. "I wouldn't want to be the window cleaner at this place."

Jane smirked. "Come on. Let's see if the priest knows anything about *I.A.*"

A black-robed man studied them from behind rimless spectacles as they approached, hands clasped behind his back. Tufts of white hair sprouted from above each ear like wings for his bald head.

"Good afternoon," he said. "Welcome."

Jane offered her hand. "Hello. I'm on the faculty at Edinburgh University, and this is my assistant. I have a question about the church."

"Certainly." Hands now resting on his ample belly, he inclined his head toward the expansive interior. "What do you wish to know?"

"We're researching the relationship between the church and Stirling's past inhabitants. Is there anyone associated with Holy Rude who has the initials *I.A.*? Our best guess is they lived here around 1700."

The priest raised an eyebrow. "A strange request." His palms turned skyward. "Is there anything else you can tell me about this person? Our history is long."

Honestly," Jane said, "we're not even certain it's a person. All we have are those two letters and the idea that they relate to this church."

The grin sparkling in his eyes blossomed. "Follow me."

The rotund holy man led them back to the main entrance. Before they stepped outside, he retrieved a stack of papers from the literature available for visitors. The door creaked open, and the priest shaded his eyes against the sunlight. "I suggest you start here." His other hand swept over the wide expanse of gravestones on the grounds and surrounding hillside. "Perhaps the person you seek rests under our Lord's sky with others who have gone to paradise."

"There are hundreds of graves here," Parker said.

"Thousands, though I have never counted." The papers he held went out to Jane. "This is a list of everyone buried in our cemetery, grouped and labeled on the map."

Parker could have kissed the guy. "Thank you. This will save us hours."

"Best of luck," the priest said as Parker grabbed Jane's arm and hustled her away.

Only once the man had gone back inside did Parker stop walking. "I'm not trying to get rid of him, but I'm trying to get rid of him. Don't need someone tagging along."

"Good call," Jane said. "Let me look at this list." Stepping under the shade of a nearby tree, she flipped the stapled pages open to the map. "It's divided into twenty-five sections. Each has a different number of plots." Her eyes whizzed across the page while Parker waited. "No fewer than one hundred per section, and some have three times that many."

"How many graves are we talking about here?"

"A few thousand." Jane stopped flipping pages and looked up. "The good news is we have a list of the people buried here."

"What's the bad news?"

"It doesn't list birth or death dates."

Parker ran a hand over his hair. "We'll have to check any grave with those initials."

Jane pulled the pages apart and handed half to him, along with a pen. "Start circling." She headed toward the far corner of the graveyard, high up a hillside behind which the sun would eventually fall. A shadow already crept over the peak, the daily curtain falling on this green patch of land. "We'll search in a grid pattern. Anybody who wasn't alive within twenty years of 1700 gets cut."

"What about the ones who were?"

She didn't look up from the paper. "I'm still working on that. Ideas would be appreciated."

He had none to offer. By the time they walked to the cemetery's corner edge, Parker had found eleven candidates, each in a different section. "How many do you have?" he asked.

"Eight possible people in six different sections. So we have to check seventeen of the twenty-five sections. Not ideal, but at least this person didn't have a more common set of initials."

"Assuming we're looking for a person." Headstones stretched into the distance. This would take days, and they might not even be on the right track. He sighed. If Erika were here, she'd have it figured out by now. She always did.

"Keep your chin up." Jane smacked his shoulder lightly. "If nothing else, it's a nice change of pace from your usual workdays."

Which have mostly been spent in the pub. "You're right. Sorry to be a downer."

"It's fine." This time her hand found his shoulder and stayed there. "You've had a hard go of things."

"No harder than others. It's the suddenness that gets to you." A deep breath, and then he pushed Erika's face from his mind. "You knew Erika. She'd be doing the same thing you are, and if I didn't get moving, it would be trouble. Lead the way, Dr. White. Time to find a gravestone."

Jane gripped his shoulder tightly before letting go. "Now," she tapped her pen on the list. "One person with the correct initials is in this section. You start on one side and I'll take the other. Meet you in the middle."

Parker stepped off with a renewed bounce in his step, and he turned to find Jane watching him. He flashed a thumbs-up. Five minutes later Jane found the first possible match. Turned out the man hadn't been born until 1805, so they crossed him off and moved on. They could clear a section in ten minutes working together, so by the time they located all nineteen graves containing people whose initials were *I.A.*, two hours had passed.

They sat on a bench under one of the thick trees; Jane bit her lip as she wrote.

"What's the final verdict?" Parker asked. "Whoever built this place could have chosen a flatter part of town. Some of those hills are steep."

"Exercise is good for us," she said.

She had a point, Parker conceded. This was the hardest workout he'd done since landing in Scotland six months earlier. The most sun he'd seen as well. Sweat coated his back, his legs ached and needles of pain pricked the grafted skin. Damn, he was out of shape.

"Out of nineteen possibilities," Jane went on, "only two fit the time frame. Innes Acklan was born in 1679 and died in 1734."

"Right in the middle," Parker said. Leaning against the backrest, he watched a tiny European car pull into the church parking lot and find a spot. "The other one?"

"Ian Armitage, born 1675, died 1706."

A pair of bicyclists cruised past on the road. The one with a picnic basket in front waved, and Parker waved back. "Both around the right time, and with the right initials. We need to check both of them."

Jane circled one name. "I think I know which person we want."

Parker raised an eyebrow. "Did I miss something? James didn't give anything but initials. No description, no other names, nothing."

"James and Philip had something in common that I think helps us narrow the search." She looked up from the paper. "James and Philip were both men. My guess is they're referencing another man as their 'compatriot'." She leaned closer to him. "You're not from Scotland, so I'm not surprised you don't know this. Innes is a girl's name." She showed him the heavy circle around *Ian Armitage*. "This is our man. James is pointing Philip to Ian's grave."

"Which means Ian died before James wrote the letter." Parker smacked his thigh. "Ian died before all this happened. The grave is a marker. You don't forget where your friends are buried." His jaw clenched. "It's a perfect clue."

"I know Erika taught you about history. Put that to use and figure this out."

His neck muscles relaxed. "Erika never taught me how to commune with the dead." Parker rubbed his hands together. "Well, maybe one way. How do you feel about breaking a minor law or two?"

Jane slipped the list into her back pocket. "Do I need my tools?"

"Better grab them. Meet you at Ian's tombstone."

Jane headed to the car. It took Parker a minute to find Ian's tomb, and by then Jane was walking back toward him, black bag in hand. A pair of men deep in conversation crossed her path, clutching flowers as they headed further into the cemetery.

"It's an interesting tombstone," Parker said. "Not in bad shape."

Time had faded the lettering slightly, though you could still make out Ian's name and his birth and death dates. The stone was carved in the shape of a cross, with an inscription running along the base. The whole structure reached no higher than Parker's waist.

"James left something here three hundred years ago. If he buried it close to ground level, it will have long since come to the surface. Rain, snow, any type of weather event makes the soil shift." He frowned at her. "I take it you didn't do much landscaping at your castle."

Jane blushed. "We had gardeners."

"Must be nice." He winked. "Things move in the ground over time if they're not buried deep. I'd find old fence posts or bricks at my parents' property after a heavy rain or in the spring."

"We should check the tombstone as well," she said.

His fingers bounced on the letters. The whole thing looked solid. "There may be a compartment or hollow portion. He used that with the baptismal bowl."

"What about the initials?" Jane crouched near the cross's base. "Could they have any significance?"

The knife came out, probing around the *I* and *A*. "Looks solid. No cracks or crevices." He checked the remaining letters and numbers without result. "Nothing here."

Jane got down low on the ground. "The base looks solid."

Shadows descended on their corner of the graveyard as passing clouds blocked the sun. When the puffy white cover moved on, the carved stone sparkled. The entire cross lit up like diamonds. Except one part.

That's weird. A thin line of stone remained dark where the top point of the cross jutted up from the horizontal portion. No sparks flashed there. He ran a finger along it. *Rougher than the rest of the cross.* "Jane?"

She looked up, pulled a lock of hair from her face. "Find something?"

"Take a look at this."

She jumped up and nearly knocked him down the hillside. "Oops."

"Look. This part of the cross doesn't sparkle in sunlight."

Jane touched where he pointed. "It's less polished here," she said, scratching the stone. Her next words were softer. "Did you find any other pieces like this?" Parker shook his head. "That's good."

"Why?"

"Hold this." The tool bag clattered off his chest. "I remember seeing this before. Give me your knife." She picked at the thin line, scratching small pebbles free as she poked. Then she put a pebble on her tongue.

"Are you *eating* that?"

"Tasting," she said before spitting it out. "What I expected. This has limestone in it."

"You can tell that by tasting it?"

"With reasonable certainty. I'd need a lab to be positive, but for now a taste works. This part of the cross is made with limestone." Jane must have noted his confusion. "Why is that important, you ask? Because in 1700, limestone was a main component of what we'd call cement."

"And cement doesn't reflect light?"

"Correct. Unlike the rest of the cross. Which begs the question: why did they need cement for this tombstone?"

Just like that, it hit him. Parker nearly dropped the tool bag. "To reattach the top *after someone broke it off*."

"Makes sense," Jane said. "James had already repaired the broken stone from the baptismal bowl. There's no reason he couldn't have repaired a damaged tombstone."

Parker glanced around. The two men who'd bumped into Jane earlier were still around. A trio of thick, leafy oaks stood between the pair and Ian's grave. Not ideal, but it would do. "Do you have a hammer?"

"Large or small?" She held up two nearly identical tools, one twice as large as the other.

"Small." Parker hefted the hammer, spun it around. "Quieter that way." Everyone other than the flower guys was far enough away that they wouldn't hear. "Stand between me and those men." Using the hammer's claw end, he gave a half-hearted swing. What could generously be described as a pebble came loose.

"Swing harder or we'll be here all night."

"Just watch for intruders." The hammer came down with a *crack*, and a much larger chunk of debris flew away. "I can see the original break. That's mortar coming off."

"Less talk, more hammer."

Parker whacked at the tombstone every few seconds, leaving enough time for the sounds to fade before attacking again. Bit by bit the mortar cracked and gave way to leave a jagged outline of broken stone above and below. Sweat beaded on his forehead. As the underused muscles in his arm began to scream and shout, he gave a decisive blow and the top of the cross shifted.

"I almost have it," he said. Jane crowded close behind him, the floral scent of her hair finding his nose on the breeze. "I think I can twist it off."

He grabbed the top portion and pushed.

"Wait," Jane nearly shouted. "You're moving the whole thing. Don't knock it over."

The entire cross had indeed shifted slightly, so Parker went back to work with the hammer until he came full circle, a narrow sliver of mortar remaining where he'd started. "Hold on a second," he said, wiping a forearm across his face. "Where can we hide the broken parts?"

"Worry about that later." Jane reached for the hammer. "Need me to take over?"

Parker gave the tombstone another whack. "That should do it," he said. "Stand back."

Gently this time, he wriggled the top portion back and forth, grit cracking and falling with each move. His leg muscles tightened as he pushed, leaning his weight into it. The stone shifted in his grasp. "Here it goes." Another push and the top fell, thumping onto the grass with scarcely a crack. Jane darted over and grabbed the piece before it rolled away.

"Do you see anything?" he asked between breaths.

"It's hollow. There's a container in here. Look at—"

"Is everything alright, Dr. White?"

The strange voice sent Parker's heart into his throat. Jane shrieked and fell over as Parker whipped around. Two men stood not ten feet away. The men carrying flowers who'd bumped into Jane.

"What? Yes, everything is fine." Jane looked up at them from the ground. "We've had an accident is all. This tombstone… Wait a moment." Her eyes narrowed. "Do I know you?"

One of the men reached into his coat. Sunlight glinted off a silver gun. "You do not." He leveled the weapon at Jane's chest. "Hand it to me."

"What are you talking about?"

"Whatever you found in the tombstone. Do not make me ask again." His flat-brimmed cap shaded his eyes as he turned the gun on Parker. "I know you and this man came here in search of something," he said, still looking at Jane. "Give it to me."

Parker's mouth opened. "You guys are—"

"Here." Jane gained her feet and stepped in front of him. "You're right. Take it, but put the gun away." The gunman grabbed the object from her hand and passed it to his friend. "Ouch." Jane pulled her hand back. "Now leave us alone."

"Do not follow us," the gunman said. "Stay here. If I see you again…" He tapped the pistol.

As the two men headed to the parking lot, Parker touched Jane's shoulder. "Are you okay?" Not once did his eyes leave the pair. He wouldn't forget their faces.

"Yes," Jane said. Brave, but a lie. She was shaking. "They had a gun, Parker. A *gun*." Jane hugged herself. "People don't carry guns here."

"You did the right thing." They watched as the men drove two separate cars out of the parking lot, one looping around the cemetery, not far from Ian's grave. "They meant business. Trust me. Giving it to them was the right move." As the car crested a hill and disappeared, he caught the license plate. *Got you.*

Out came his phone. "We'll see what Nick has to say about those two."

Jane tugged at her hair. "Who's Nick?"

"A friend." Parker slipped the phone back into his pocket. "I got one license plate. If he's any good at being a bad guy, chances are it won't pan out. Still, you never know."

"Is Nick a policeman?"

"Of a sort." He scooped up her bag. "Come on, let's get out of here. A drink would do wonders right now."

Jane stopped tugging her hair. "You want to leave?"

He did a double take. "You don't? Jane, those men would have shot us. Apart from that, they took the message. We can't keep going, even if we wanted to."

"You're right. They have one of the messages."

"*One* of them?"

She reached down her shirt and fished around. "Yes. The one from back at Melrose Abbey." She held out a small, dingy metal tube. "Not the one James left here. That one I kept."

His legs tingled at the sight of what looked like a metal pill container. "When you fell down. You stuck it inside your shirt."

"Those two didn't notice. I handed them an old piece of leather with writing on it." She shrugged. "Why wouldn't they believe I found it here?"

Wasn't Jane just full of surprises? Thinking fast with a gun trained on her, and now they were still ahead of the bad guys. "Let's get out of here before those two come back. I'll drive while you figure out what that is. Harder for them if we keep moving."

They made it to his car unscathed, passing several visitors who had no idea that an armed robbery and tombstone desecration had just occurred nearby. The first thing Parker did was lock the doors. Taking streets at random, he gunned it through a yellow light and doubled back twice before parking outside the local police station.

"If they're following us, I don't see them."

Jane pulled a pair of needle-nose pliers out of her tool kit. "This tube sounds hollow. Listen." She tapped the tube. "And one end is capped. So much time outside rusted it shut. We may have to rip it off."

"Just get it open."

The discolored metal shrieked once or twice, but in the end, Jane came out on top as the cap slid off. "Turn the light on." When he flicked the dome light to life, Jane grunted. "Good. I didn't risk our lives for nothing." She removed a rolled brown parchment that looked like the first message. "Good thing James used leather again."

"Is there writing?"

"Patience, Mr. Chase. What do you say we move on before reading it?"

His tires chirped as they scooted back into traffic. Jane put her tools away and laid a square of white cloth across her lap. "Not ideal protection, but it will do. Try to be easy with the brakes."

"Before you do that, we need to talk about what just happened."

"I'm fine. It may hit me later, but right now I feel great." She held up their find. "We're still on the trail. This is fantastic."

"It's not that, although I'm glad you're all right. How did those two find us? They knew your name."

"I didn't think of that. Only a few people knew I was in Stirling. I called the department on our way. You heard me."

He recalled the brief conversation detailing their trip. "You had to get approval for the travel."

"Tom is a stickler about our accounts. He gets cranky if I don't clear travel beforehand." Parker raised an eyebrow. "You think *Tom* is involved?" She laughed. "There's no one less likely to know thugs with guns than Tom Gregan."

"If you say so. Who else knew?"

Jane started ticking off names on her fingers. "Evan, my grad assistant. Hugh, of course."

The old caretaker. He liked that guy. "I doubt Hugh is selling you out."

"Once I tell him what happened, it will be all we can do to keep him from hunting them down," Jane said. Her brow furrowed. "Other than those three, no one knew about this trip."

"Would they have told other people?"

"I'm not sure Hugh knows anyone to tell," she said. "He doesn't have any family, and he spends his free time at the library or gardening."

"What about colleagues?"

"Perhaps in conversation. Our schedules aren't a secret." She snapped her fingers. "In fact, they're posted on an internal site. The university has a shared calendar for all faculty and staff showing who is on campus and when."

"Does it say where people are when they're not on campus?"

"It depends. I can check when we get back to see what Tom wrote."

Sirens blared as a police car barreled past with lights flashing. He nearly rear-ended the car ahead. "If Tom listed your destination, hundreds of people could have known where you were going to be. That's less than helpful." That meant people she likely didn't know could track her. Or share what they knew with others. Narrowing down the list would be impossible. Parker pulled into an open spot by the sidewalk and took a deep breath. "We'll worry about that when we get back to Edinburgh."

"Fair enough." She picked up the miniature scroll and unrolled it with exaggerated care. Air whistled between her teeth. "It's the same handwriting as before."

Familiar black script appeared. He leaned over the center console and read the next stage of James's journey.

Philip,

I suspect Ian would have been delighted to play a role in our endeavor. I have evaded pursuit thus far. I have my plain satchel in tow, carrying the three pillars on which our faith rests.

Trust that my strange path is done to keep Scotland's honour safe. I now travel to kneel with, and beneath, the wooden gaze of England's royal reformer. Behind this you must go.

James

All vagueness and mystery. At least James hadn't been caught yet. "Talk about confusing," Parker said. "James must have been worried about someone else finding the message. It's one big riddle."

"Unless you have the key," Jane said.

"This makes sense to you?"

"Hardly." Her eyes darted over the impossibly neat text. "It's like each sentence hints at what he really wants to say. 'Three pillars'.

'Kneel with and beneath'. 'Wooden gaze'. None of it means much to me."

"That's better than the big bag of nothing I got from it," he said. "Unless those three pillars are the smallest ever made, I don't know how he's carrying them around."

"Good question. One of many." She frowned and held her chin. "Only one part is clear." Jane tapped the page. "Right here. 'England's royal reformer'. He's talking about Henry VIII."

"The guy with all the wives?" Jane said it was. "Was he from Scotland?"

"No. Plus, Henry VIII died a hundred and fifty years before we think these letters were written."

"How do you know he's the 'reformer' James mentions?"

"When Henry decided his first marriage to Catherine of Aragon should be annulled, he needed the Catholic church's blessing. By church, I mean the Pope. The Pope wasn't keen on annulling any marriage, king or not. So, Henry did what most powerful men do when they don't get their way. He changed the rules."

"He told the Pope to go pound salt."

"Better than that," she said. "He initiated the English Reformation. Avoiding the dogmatic details, he basically said the Pope wasn't in charge of Henry's new church. Henry was. As the boss, Henry could annul his own marriage, and that's what happened. Catherine went away, leaving Henry free to eventually marry Anne Boleyn after he finished having an affair with her sister Mary."

A diesel engine roared as a delivery truck motored past. Parker leaned back in his seat, churning through each piece of this increasingly intricate puzzle. *Think logically.* How many times had Erika told him you don't have to be a historian to find a solution to a history problem. It wasn't history when it happened. It was real life, with real people. People who thought like he did.

"Does Henry VIII have any connection to Stirling?" he asked.

"Good question. There's nothing I'm aware of, although it's

possible he visited the area." She snapped her fingers. "There's someone I know who could tell us more about this place than I can." She grabbed her phone. "Evan Ford is from Stirling. Part of his dissertation effort involves the city."

While Jane spoke with Evan and explained what was going on, Parker pulled out his phone and opened the car door. He held up a finger in answer to Jane's questioning look. *One minute.* The buttery scent of leather whisked away when he stepped out, diesel's pungent embrace grabbing his nose and not letting go. He dodged a gray-haired woman being led around by two dogs and slid into the shadow of a narrow building.

Leaning against the building, which turned out to be a pub, of course, Parker pressed the phone to his ear. Beeps and clicks stretched on as a phone rang somewhere in America. At least he suspected his friend was in the States. *Come on, Nick. I could use a little help right now.*

A gruff voice broke the silence. "Nick Dean."

"Nick, it's Parker."

"I thought you crawled into a hole and disappeared. An expensive hole, probably. Damn, Parker, what's it been, five months now?"

"Since the funeral."

Nick coughed. "Yes. Since the funeral." Parker waited, the silence stretching on. "A moving service," Nick finally said. "I know Erika would have approved."

"Thanks. You have a minute?"

"What's on your mind?"

Where to start? As near the end as possible. Fewer questions that way. "I need to find out who owns a car. I ran into trouble with someone."

"Are you talking felony or misdemeanor trouble?"

"Not even a summary offense. It's nothing, really. More of a precaution."

"You sure about that?" Parker said he was. "Okay, give me the tag, state first."

Oops. "It's a Scottish tag. As in the country."

"I heard you'd left the States."

"How did you know I left?" He hadn't mentioned his plans to Nick or anyone else. He hadn't even known what he planned to do other than get away from Pennsylvania, the farther the better.

"Better you don't ask," Nick said with a laugh. "Keeping tabs on a civilian isn't hard, but it's also not exactly legal. Unless you're committing espionage, of course."

"All your CIA resources. I guess you wouldn't be much of an agent if you couldn't keep track of me." Based in Philadelphia, Nick was part of a specialized task force operating on American soil. His team liaised with domestic federal intelligence in an off-the-books operation outside traditional jurisdictions. As Nick had said more than once, "We actually get things done without the bullshit."

"The job has its perks. Give me the tags and anything else you have on the car." Parker rattled off the plate number he'd seen along with a vehicle description. "There was another guy involved, but I didn't get anything on him."

"Sounds like you're making lots of friends over there." Keyboard clicks sounded in Parker's ear, and Nick whistled tunelessly. "Give me a few hours," he said. "I know a guy. I'll run it past him and send you what I find."

"Thanks, Nick. I appreciate it."

"No problem," Nick said. "Now you have to do me a favor."

"What's that?"

"I know what kind of trouble you get in without Erika around to save your butt. Keep your eyes open and head down."

"I'll do my best." He clicked off, the government agent's words still ringing in his ears. Not that long ago he and Erika had saved Nick's life, and Nick had later returned the favor. When they had spoken at her funeral, an undercurrent of tension had run through Nick's condolences, and Parker had been puzzled.

"Everything okay?" Jane asked when he slid back into the car.

"Fine. I called the guy who can get information about one of the men in the cemetery. He's looking into it."

"Useful friend. What kind of man can do that?"

"A government guy. I helped him out before."

Jane's eyes narrowed to slits. "Do better than that," she said. "They had a *gun*, Parker."

What the hell. Here goes nothing. "You're not going to believe me." She didn't budge. "Fine. Erika and I saved this man's life once. His name is Nick, and he works for the CIA."

Her mouth turned into an oval. "You're joking." He assured her he wasn't. "How in the world did you save his life?"

"The short version is some men wanted us dead, and Nick was already investigating them. We happened to be around to help. After that we were in it together, and from then on we've been buddies." He'd left out the interesting parts, but that was the gist of it.

"Erika was involved too?" Parker nodded. "How did that happen?"

He put his hands up. "I'll tell you more later. We have a new problem to worry about now."

Jane's mouth hardened. "Only if you tell me about Erika and Ireland."

His head jerked up. "You know what happened. A bomb exploded beneath our car—"

"I know *how* it happened. Not *why*."

Tell her about Erika's murder? He'd never spoken to anyone about it. "We'll see. What did Evan say?"

She blinked, and the present came rushing back. "I was right; he's done research on his hometown. Loads of it. When I asked about connections Henry VIII had with Stirling, he knew right off." She showed him a piece of paper with scribbling on it. "Records don't show any visits of note from Henry, though it's possible he spent time in Stirling at one point or another. No major church renovations or vanity buildings. However," and here her face lit up, "Evan reminded me about the Stirling Heads at Stirling Castle."

"I hope you're not talking about actual heads."

"No," she said. "These are meter-wide oak medallions depicting royalty, Roman emperors and other people."

"Any English royalty?"

"Good guess. Not all of the original carvings are still around. They were on the ceiling of James V's bedroom, until part of the castle collapsed in 1777." She consulted her notes. "Lucky for us, not only is Henry VIII one of the carvings, his original still exists."

"If the collapse happened in 1777, the carvings were still on the ceiling when James wrote his message." Parker rubbed his unusually smooth chin. "But how did James expect Philip to get to a carving in the king's bedroom? And how can we do it?"

Jane coughed. "The carvings aren't on a ceiling now. They're on display in a gallery."

"Is that a problem?"

"Displays mean security," Jane said. "They won't take kindly to visitors messing with the artifacts."

"You think our next marker is the wood carving."

Jane shrugged. "That's my guess."

Parker buckled his seat belt and put the Mustang in gear. "Then we find it, security or not." He whipped into traffic before she could answer and headed across town toward the sprawling castle. Perched on the highest ground in sight, steep cliffs surrounded it on three sides.

"You grew up in a castle," he said. "Any secrets to share?"

"Yes and no." She didn't look at him when she answered. "We just had a big, old house, and so did all my friends."

"Erika mentioned your parents were nobles."

"As minor as they come," she said. "My father's family lived in the castle for generations. He inherited it long before I was born. Then he met a much younger woman, and I happened." One finger twisted a lock of hair as she spoke, rolling it in endless circles. "I'm an only child. My leaving for university didn't help their relationship."

"The empty nest was too quiet?"

"I suppose. Everything I know came from Hugh, and he keeps things close to the chest." She fell silent, the engine burbling while they waited at a traffic light. "My parents were both very British."

"Stiff upper lip kind of folks."

"Exactly. Problems aren't to be shared; soldier on, old boy; that whole thing. I wasn't shocked when my father told me they were separating. Affection between them was formal. They were wonderful parents," she said hurriedly. "I never felt unloved. A rift simply formed between them when I wasn't looking, I suppose."

"I'm sorry. Divorce is hard on children."

Jane stared out the window. "Yes, it is." The signal changed, and forward movement jolted her back to life. "Father is in England, Mother in France, and I'm living in a drafty castle having the time of my life with an American." Her face lit up with a real smile. "Right now, I wouldn't rather be anywhere else."

Parker raised his hand from the shift knob and she slapped it. "That's the spirit. Now, tell me those castle secrets."

"I know one: have lots of money and firewood if you want to stay warm. Seriously, though, other than that I don't have any special insight. Every castle I've been to is different."

"How many are we talking about here? Did you have play dates with other castle-dwellers?"

"Old homes are more common in Scotland," she said. "And yes, some of our family friends also had stone homes with rooms to spare. Each one is unique. Some even have hidden passageways between rooms, like ours."

He shot her a look. "You have secret passages? That's awesome."

"From the main hall to the master bedroom, and from my father's study to the basement. Of course, I didn't know this until I was older. It explained why I never once won a game of hide-and-seek."

Parker turned on to a winding two-lane road. Hitting the gas, he motored up the hill, mirrors perilously close to a stone retaining wall on one side. "No other secrets to share. Bummer. I guess we have to figure this out on our own."

"It's worked so far," Jane said. "Any secrets about Stirling Castle were uncovered long ago. As for my house, I remember when Hugh uncovered some old carvings which had been covered over. Stone chaps in armor cut into the wall no one had ever seen. He found it when a patch of masonry collapsed. We found an entire scene on the wall."

"Let's hope anything that was around when James came through still exists. Otherwise we're stuck, and I don't want to wait for those thugs to realize you gave them an old clue."

Jane was silent, hands clenched together in her lap, the knuckles going white.

The road funneled them toward the castle grounds. Buildings on either side dropped off suddenly as they moved, as though the ground had been cleaved away on each side. Beyond the sudden cliffs the River Forth sparkled between thick trees, a wealth-generating trade route in centuries past over which the castle offered unchallenged dominion.

"We're not the only ones visiting today," Parker said when a mostly full parking lot appeared ahead. "More people means more chances to distract the guards."

"Or to get caught," Jane said, though she didn't hesitate when Parker got out and headed for the entrance. "We only have a few hours. Whatever there is to find here, we need to do it quickly."

"I'm working on a plan," Parker said. He paid the entrance fee, passing beneath an expansive stone arch and into the main grounds. A small child raced by with two parents in hot pursuit. Bird poop splattered beside his foot, and Jane pulled hers out of the danger zone. "What else do you know about this place?"

"Not as much as I should," she said. "It dates to the tenth

century, though the oldest buildings standing today were built hundreds of years after that."

"After James and Philip's time?"

"I'd say fourteenth century, depending on which section you're talking about." She pulled a crumpled page of notes from her pocket. "Most of the main structures were built a hundred years before James came here."

They passed a pair of employees leaning against a building, paying the guests no attention. "Any idea where to go?"

"The Royal Palace," she said. "Follow me."

Dodging around other visitors who seemed to stop and admire every stone and speck of dirt, they passed buildings made from dark stone and darker mortar before he spotted a promising sign.

"Here we go. *Stirling Heads Gallery.*" Jane kept pace as he walked inside and turned a corner, where a tiny suit of armor caught his eye. "Look how small it is. Must have been made for a child."

"It belonged to James V."

"I thought you didn't know much about this place?"

"I don't." She pointed to a placard beside the armor. "The card told me."

"Oh. Good eyes." *Nice one, doofus.* "The king was a little guy."

"People were a lot smaller then," she said. "You would have been considered massive."

He didn't consider a few inches north of six feet *massive.* "Being big just means the archers have a bigger target. Give me hard-to-hit any day." Jane actually laughed at that one. She was warming up, back in her element, out in the field. "Tell me about these carvings. Did Evan's research mention any legends or stories? Those can be good starting points."

"There's nothing unusual about the carvings. They're oak, each about three feet wide."

The castle modernized as they moved deeper inside. Exterior stone walls gave way to drywall, while wood beams blackened with age intermixed with newer vaulted ceilings and soft spotlights. A sign pointed him to the correct room.

"I think we found it," he said.

"You should have been a detective." Jane pushed past him, grinning at the castle employee standing outside as she walked. The guy beamed from ear to ear.

"Way to be subtle," Parker whispered when he caught up to her. "That kid won't forget you for a while."

"I can't help it that he has good taste."

Score one for Jane. "Fair enough. Where is King Henry?"

Jane stopped in front of the first display case. Glass fronted the free-standing wall on which hung two carvings, neither of them Henry VIII. More displays lined up behind this one, and others ran the length of the opposite wall. Arms crossed on her chest, Jane studied the oak circles for scarcely a second before moving on. "Look." She pointed to the glass covering each display. "It's not fully covered. There's a space between the glass and the carvings."

Set several feet in front of the carvings on display, each glass barrier left enough room for a person to fit inside. A person much skinnier than Parker. "I can't fit in there."

"I can." She twisted, and sure enough her shoulders fit between the glass cover and the carving. "Let's hope Henry isn't between two other ones."

"I hope whatever James left for Philip is in plain sight," Parker said. "That security guard won't like you so much if you touch the display." He followed her into the next aisle to find another pair of visitors speaking softly as they admired carvings depicting mythological figures. Parker moved on to find nobles and Roman emperors, but no Henry. He glanced back and couldn't see the guard standing watch. *If I can't see him, he can't see us.*

"Parker." Jane's voice carried a sense of urgency. "Get over here."

He moved over to find her back in front of the display case again. "I found him." A bearded wooden man looked back at them through the glass, no crown on his head nor scepter in hand. None of his wives joined him in the circular frame, though the king wasn't alone.

"Is that a lion on his shoulders?" Parker asked.

"It is. The lion has long been associated with England. In the Middle Ages lions were kept at the Tower of London. There's also Richard the Lionheart, and if you're a football fan, the national team is often called the Three Lions."

The two visitors from a moment earlier appeared beside them, one clutching a guide map to her chest. "We should go to the Chapel Royal after this," she said. "I read the new paintings are beautiful."

Parker and Jane waited until they moved on. "Think the lion has anything to do with the message?" Parker asked.

"Not unless it had personal meaning for James and Philip. If that's the case, we're in trouble." Jane pulled out her phone. "It's dark in here and I can't see these clearly. My first thought is a message of some kind *on* the carving. He could have made a mark that we just can't see right now."

"Made a mark when it was hanging on the ceiling? How would he do that?"

"The precise timeline of when these carvings moved from the ceiling to another part of the castle isn't certain. It could be they fell before James came through, or maybe it was hanging on a wall. Or James could have gotten into the building and left a message. Or he had friends who helped."

"Are we making the facts fit our theory?" Parker asked.

"Only one way to find out," Jane said. Her lips pursed as she studied the carving.

Nothing on it stood out. No letters or insignias. When another tourist paused in their aisle, Jane put her phone away, waiting for them to leave.

"I don't see anything on the front," she said.

"We can only see half of it." He checked the door. Still no sign of the guard. "You want to go in while I keep an eye out for company?"

"I can slip in there and kneel down to get a view of the backside." She dipped as though tying her shoe. "There's almost a foot of clearance between the bottom of it and the wall."

"If James scratched a message into the backside, wouldn't someone have seen it by now?"

"Only one way to find out." Parker's chest tightened as though a band had wrapped around it. Without the next message, the path ended. "Keep your eyes open," Jane said. With that, she slipped into the display case.

She stumbled, and her nose flattened along the inside of the glass, leaving a smudge they'd be hard-pressed to explain. Parker kept one eye on the front entrance and one on Jane. It seemed to take an eternity, though it was only a few seconds before she knelt and slipped under the massive wooden circle.

She banged against the glass and nearly wedged herself in place. By sliding sideways she'd managed to get into the opening, but she couldn't twist around to get a good look. A palm-print remained when she steadied herself.

Voices rang from the hallway. Parker tapped the glass. *Wait.* He stepped to the door, cocking an ear toward the hallway to catch a muffled conversation.

"Excuse me, sir," said a man's voice. "Would you point me to the loo?"

The security man obliged with directions, and as the footsteps faded Parker moved back inside, flashing a thumbs-up. Jane wriggled around, contorting into a semi-crouch to catch a view of the carving's backside. After a brief struggle to grab her phone, the flashlight came on and she held it up.

The security guard's radio crackled to life down the hallway. Between the static and the thick accents, Parker couldn't make any sense of the exchange, but the guard never moved and silence soon returned. Turning back toward Jane, he looked up and came face-to-face with a security guard coming through the other entrance.

Parker's chest seized up. The guard offered a grin. "Good evening," he said. "The castle will be closing in one hour. Please keep this in mind."

The guard stood inches from the display. Shadows danced on the ground as Jane twisted around inside the case with her flashlight. One swept over the guard's shoe. He didn't notice.

"Sir, are you okay?" The guard stepped forward. "Is anything wrong?"

"No, I'm fine." Parker cracked the ice on his frozen muscles and stepped aside, giving the guard room to pass. "Sorry."

"I hope you enjoy the castle," the guard said, and Parker nodded as he brushed past. A wrenching squeaking noise filled the air, as though a massive windshield wiper had rubbed across dry glass. Both men turned in time to see Jane tumble in a heap beneath Henry VIII.

"I think she's hurt," Parker said, pulling the guard along with him. "We have to get her out of there. You go around the other side." The guard's mouth opened, then closed again as he hurried to the far end and out of sight.

"Get up fast." Parker whispered through clenched teeth. Jane scrambled around, making it worse and getting nowhere in her haste.

"Are you injured, miss?" the guard called. Jane didn't respond. "Miss, what are you doing in there?"

She stood sideways and started to wriggle out. Her foot caught, and she took out Henry VIII's disc on her way down. It landed with a booming crash, rolling toward the security guard and hitting another carving.

"Move!" Parker reached into the gap and grabbed for Jane's hand.

"Stop moving," the guard shouted, fumbling for the radio at his waist.

Parker grabbed Jane's arm and pulled. Six months ago, he could have lifted her off her feet, but now all he managed to do was drag her out of the display case and send them both sprawling. Parker scrambled to his feet and sprinted away, Jane following him as the security guard radioed for assistance. Parker turned the corner and cut through the first doorway he found, bursting into the middle of an ancient stag hunt. Massive tapestries lined the walls and groups of tourists huddled in front of the scenes of vivid green forests and stylish courtiers chasing unicorns and deer with leashed hounds. No one noticed the two disheveled guests who walked rapidly past.

More doors lined the walls of this room. Parker picked one and raced into a narrow hall. An open door waited ahead, red sunlight coloring the floor. A head appeared in the doorway for an instant, no more than a black circle backlit by the falling sun, only to vanish as Parker burst outside to find a teenager lying on the pavement.

"Excuse us," he shouted as the teenager sat up, dazed. Pain stabbed his side, a hot knife twisting through underused muscles as his lungs tightened. Jane whizzed by, leading him on their race to any place but here. *If we get out of this, I'm going back to the gym.*

The guard chasing them seemed to be losing ground. They'd nearly run across the courtyard before two more guards made it outside, only to collide with the dusty teenager, who was trying to scramble to his feet. Jane turned a corner, skidding across the slick, ancient stones into cooler shade.

"In there," she said, pointing to an oversized single-story building. Pedestrian paths extended beyond either side of the building, more choices to confuse the guards.

Parker glimpsed a plaque showing they'd entered the Chapel Royal as the rounded entranceway flashed above them. Stone turned to wood beneath his feet and the ceiling soared overhead, great panels stretching three stories high. Sunlight bathed everything. Parallel stairways descended to a lower level on either side, each blocked by a rope.

"Down there." Parker pointed to a stairwell. "We can wait until they move on and then get out of here." Jane followed him over the rope and down a staircase past several massive paintings. As the cool darkness enveloped them, the stairwell seemed eerily silent after their frantic race to freedom. Parker gulped air, his heart thundering.

"If we are caught it's my fault," he said between breaths. "I wasn't watching the other entrance."

Jane wasn't even breathing hard. "I slipped," she whispered. "It was my fault."

The wooden disc. "Did you see anything?"

"No. I didn't have much time, but there isn't anything on that disc. No marks, no letters."

Pounding footsteps cut them off, then the sound of voices. Parker's throat tightened when someone stomped into the chapel, breathing heavily. Whoever it was ran to the far side, away from them.

"Against the wall," Parker whispered. They pressed their backs to the stones. A thick brass guiderail offered slight cover from above, and the shadows stretched deep into the staircase. Boots clomped over and a head flashed into the light above them.

Parker's chest burned. He didn't breathe, didn't move.

"All clear!" The head vanished, the footsteps faded, and Parker gulped in sweet air. Jane touched a finger to her lips as she moved past him. A glance around, and she wordlessly motioned for him to follow.

"I don't think they're waiting outside," she whispered. "I heard footsteps running off. Wait another minute."

Fine with him. Let those guards chase shadows while they escaped. Parker stayed slumped against the stairs, the wooden ceiling above seeming to glow in the dying sunlight. Its dark wood was like burnt umber come to life. The sun's rays caught the upper half of a painting above them, glistening in the man's full beard. The painting was huge, well over ten feet high. Whoever had hung that had better have done a good job, he thought gloomily, because if it fell, they'd be cut in half. The man portrayed in it was taller than him, and the wood cross supporting it stretched higher still.

Parker's eyes grew tight. *That face looks familiar. And the cross – it's brown. Like the trees outside.*

He grabbed Jane's arm. "What did the note say about Henry VIII? His '*wooden gaze*', wasn't it?"

"'*I travel to kneel with, and beneath, the wooden gaze of England's royal reformer. Behind this you must go.*' The carved heads are oak," she said. "It's the only thing that makes sense inside Stirling Castle."

"What if he wasn't talking about the carvings?" Parker leaned farther back against the wall to get a better view. "James could have meant a different Henry."

"What?" She hadn't looked directly at him yet, still watching for guards. "I think we can go. We passed an exit by—"

"I'm talking about this." He pointed up. "Recognize that guy?"

She blinked twice, hard. "That's Henry."

Bigger than life, sporting a full beard, Henry looked down on the entire room with an inscrutable expression. There was no lion in sight this time, but a different object caught Parker's attention. "Look at the cross beside him. What's it made of?"

"Any cross that size had to be made of...*wood*." She latched on to his wrist. "It's made of wood. Do you think—"

"—that's what he meant by *wooden gaze*? Yes, I do. It makes sense." Parker ticked mental boxes. "This painting was more accessible than the carvings. It may have been moved here from anywhere in the castle."

"Which means it's possible James saw this," Jane said. "Paintings this large had more than one purpose. To honor the subject, but also to remind people of power, and who held it. This image of Henry reminded everyone who came here that the Crown controlled Scotland."

Parker checked the chapel; nobody in sight. "So where's the message?"

"James described kneeling beneath the wooden gaze. Maybe he's detailing what you'd see while kneeling in front of the painting. He could be talking about the frame."

"Do you think that's the original frame?" Parker asked.

"Only one way to find out." She favored him with a sharp glance, as though he were a painting and she the critic. "How strong is your back?"

"Strong enough to lift you, I suppose."

"Don't drop me." Jane slipped out of her shoes. "Now kneel." He did, and she clambered onto his shoulders, Parker wrapping a hand around each ankle. "Stand up. *Slowly.*"

Thigh muscles shouting, he stood from the crouch until Jane's chest came level with the frame's bottom. "See anything?"

"It's likely the original frame. Hold steady." Her hands scrabbled across the wall and her weight shifted. "Same over here. There are small scratches and gouges, so I don't think it's been repaired."

All well and good, but not what they were looking for. "Anything from James?"

"Hold on," she said. Pain knifed through his shoulders and a bead of sweat formed on his brow. Eventually her weight shifted back, and Jane sighed. "I don't see anything."

"Could he be talking about a different part of the painting?" Parker asked. All he wanted to do was set her down, but this was their last hope. "If the painting was at ground level you wouldn't be looking at the frame."

"Paintings aren't normally displayed on the ground," Jane said. "People could damage them. But I'll check. Can you stand on your toes?"

Parker rose up, and his calves joined the protest. What was she doing, memorizing it? After waiting for what felt like ten minutes, he risked a question. "Any luck?"

"Not yet. I'm looking at the background." Her weight shifted again, and Parker nearly lost his balance. "Whoa," she said. "Steady. Right now, all I see is the castle behind Henry. I think it's part of Stirling Castle, so this may have been painted here. There are statues along the outer wall, a bunch of knights lined up. There's nothing..." Her voice trailed off.

"What did you say?" He sank onto his heels. "I didn't hear you."

"Stand back up."

She's got some nerve. "What's going on up there? I'm getting tired."

"This knight."

Night? "What about this night?"

"No, not night-and-day night. Knight in shining armor. There are statues of them behind Henry, outside the castle."

"So?"

"One of them is *kneeling*. The one right beside Henry's beard." She leaned forward, and he nearly tumbled back. "Lift me higher."

"This is as high as I go. Push up on your toes." He immediately regretted it, as her feet dug deeper. "Well?"

"I found it." Her phone clicked once, twice. "Set me down."

Jane came down a whole lot faster than she had gone up. Once her feet hit the steps, Parker collapsed onto his backside. "This better be right."

Jane stuck her phone in his face. "Look," she said.

He wiped sweat out of his eyes and squinted. "It's a knight. A statue of one. Like you said, he's kneeling."

"Look *behind* him."

His gaze shifted to the castle wall beside the statue. "That looks like a letter." Hair rose on his arms. "It's a '*P*'."

"Exactly." She helped him to his feet. "Think about the message. *'I travel to kneel with, and beneath, the wooden gaze of England's royal reformer. Behind this you must go.'* This is what he's talking about. It's all here. This knight is kneeling, the cross is wooden, and Henry VIII is the royal reformer." She clapped with machine-gun quickness and jumped in place. "We have to find this kneeling knight statue somewhere outside Stirling Castle."

Reality's cold rain smothered his burning enthusiasm. "We can't stay here," he said. "Those guards are looking for us."

"That's a problem." Jane sat down beside him. "We need disguises."

"Disguises?"

"Hats and sunglasses. And new clothes."

Parker shrugged. "If we come back tomorrow with all that, we could probably slip in here unnoticed. Only two guards got a good look at us."

"We're not leaving." She stood and hopped up the steps, pausing at the top. "Get up. No one else is here now."

This girl had no idea how much trouble she was asking for. They crept to the entrance and scanned outside. No guards. "How are we going to change our looks?" Parker asked. "The gift shop?"

Jane leaned back out of the sunlight. "My first thought was the lost-and-found, but we need clothes that fit."

A smile touched his lips before dying under her stare. "You're serious."

"Erika mentioned once how you earn a nice living. So go buy a few souvenirs."

"To the gift shop." Air whistled between his teeth. "Fine. Where is it? They're closing soon."

"The gift shop is always near an exit." Moving with an assurance Parker didn't share, Jane led the way, hugging the walls. They kept their eyes away from anyone they passed. No guards crossed their path, and in twenty minutes Parker walked out of the shop sporting a new hat, shirt and sunglasses. The Stirling Castle logo covered everything. He'd rolled his pants halfway up the calf at Jane's insistence, though what good that did, he couldn't tell.

"I look like a fool."

"If a flood comes through, you'll be one step ahead." He couldn't tell for sure, not behind her oversized sunglasses and wide-brimmed hat, but she might have laughed. "You look like a tourist, not a trespasser. Stop complaining and move. Time's running short."

In the gift shop they'd also picked up a map of the grounds, and after consulting the sales clerk, Jane pinpointed their kneeling knight. Set among a row of statues along the east façade of the royal palace, the knight had stood watch since the mid-sixteenth century, long before James and Philip's time. Parker and Jane again kept to the shadows and walls, moving among passing tour guides and visitors until they reached their target.

"Are you thinking to check the stonework again?" Parker asked. The kneeling knight jutted out from the castle wall several feet, rising nearly to Parker's shoulders. Seven-foot-tall knights waited farther down either side.

"Yes. Let's assume James kept to a pattern." She grabbed his shoulders and twisted him around, away from the knight. "I have a job you'll be good at. Stand there and don't move. If you see anyone paying too much attention to us, tell me and then act like you're taking my picture. You know, like normal tourists."

"How's this?" Feet spread wide, he held the shopping bag open in front of him and studied the sparse crowds from behind his over-priced shades.

"You're a natural," Jane said.

The minutes passed with agonizing slowness. When a lone staff member strolled by to remind them the museum was closing in fifteen minutes, Parker jumped into action, pretending to snap Jane's picture. She didn't blink, turning back to her search and leaving Parker to study the dwindling crowd. It wasn't hard to imagine every one of them knew what they were doing.

She didn't understand the risks, Parker realized uneasily. Maybe she'd never seen what a gun could do. Cold fire ached in his skin graft, and Parker rubbed it to no effect, looking up when Jane finally spoke.

"Is anyone watching us?"

"There's hardly anyone here," he said. The sun now came at a hard angle, most of it below the horizon. He covered his eyes. "I don't see anyone looking at us." In truth he couldn't see much of anything. "We pretty much have the place to ourselves. You find something?"

"Come back here," she said. Parker took one last look at the empty grounds. "Get out your knife," Jane said, and pointed at the wall. "You see this?"

"I see a mossy stone."

Moss tumbled when Jane scrubbed her fingers across the stone, and Parker drew in a sharp breath. "That's a letter." The jagged *P* was undeniable. He squinted. "Does the mortar look different around it?"

"Hard to say," Jane said. "This didn't have protection from the elements, so it could just be weathered. Start digging. We have less than five minutes. I'll keep watch."

He dug into the mortar, dislodging chunks with abandon. The material crumbled easily, and in short order the stone shifted, a small movement that grew with each stab until it broke free from the wall.

"Got it." Sweat dripped into his eyes and he blinked away the burn. He'd broken through into a deep hole the sunlight didn't penetrate. Pushing thoughts of snakes and crawling bugs from his head, he reached in and promptly smashed his fingers against the next layer of stone, but not before he brushed something else. Something hard. Parker fumbled around and pulled a rusted metal box into the sunlight.

The rock went back into place as he dropped the box into their shopping bag. About the size of a deck of cards, it didn't weigh much. "Just in time, too." He nodded to a pair of staff making their way through the yard, stopping by each remaining guest before pointing to the exit.

"What is it?" Jane grabbed for the bag.

Parker shook his head. "We can check in the car."

She snatched the bag this time, jumping once as they walked. "We found his trail."

He couldn't stop the smirk. "Don't tell me you lost hope."

"A little worried is all," Jane said.

When she laughed, Parker looked at her, and with the sun sparkling off her hair, he saw Erika. Not really her, of course, but her image, all the enthusiasm and joy she'd brought to every day reincarnated in an old friend. *Stop it. She's gone.* Holding on to her like this wasn't healthy. She was dead and nothing could bring her back.

Jane frowned. "Are you okay?"

"I'm fine." Parker rolled his neck. When she returned his smile, he really did feel better. They turned a corner, moving with the sparse crowd, and he almost ran into someone. "Sorry," Parker said, dodging around the man he'd nearly rear-ended. The guy didn't respond, just kept moving. *Jeez, buddy. It was an accident.*

His features were hidden beneath the brim of his green cap; he was probably one of the countless Celtic soccer fans in the area. A thought danced around the edges of his memory; this was the second green ballcap he'd seen recently, though he couldn't remember where he'd seen the first for the life of him.

"Keep up," Jane said, and when he looked up, she was nearly to the exit.

"Coming," he said, jogging to catch up. "I think we're clear."

Jane didn't look convinced, but he was proven right when they strolled through an exit alongside a mother with two children racing to eat their ice cream before it melted. The sticky trio peeled off, leaving Parker and Jane alone.

"Is anyone following us?" Jane asked as they headed for his car.

He looked back. "Just other tourists." He touched Jane's arm as she reached into the shopping bag. "Hold off for now. Once we get on the road back to Edinburgh you can have at it. You never know if those two guards patrol the parking lot."

An idling tour bus rumbled nearby. Parker had to zig between other parked cars to get to his door, and as he did, a green hat flashed at the corner of his vision. The same green from earlier. Same hat, same guy he'd nearly run over, now headed for him. The guy's head was still down, and when he turned on a direct line for Parker, it hit him.

The hat. One of the men who'd confronted them at Holy Rude. That same man was now twenty feet away.

Parker grabbed Jane's shoulder. "Run." He pushed her in the opposite direction and took off toward the man. His overworked legs found a speed he'd thought lost as he buzzed past bumpers and fenders, racing toward the man in the green hat, who still kept his eyes on the ground. If he was wrong, he'd be in jail, no question. Five steps away, and the guy didn't notice. Parker balled one hand into a fist. Two steps away, Green Hat looked up.

He wasn't wrong.

A pistol came out of the guy's pocket. Parker got low, put his shoulder out, and exploded into the man. Their bodies collided and lightning flashed across his vision as he slammed Green Hat and sent the gun flying. They both crashed into a parked car, luckily with Green Hat between him and the metal body to soften the blow. Metal crumpled as they slid across the hood, and the back of Parker's mind registered a distant scream. Was that Jane?

Green Hat and Parker crashed together onto the asphalt hard enough that Parker let go. The guy bounced off a tire, kicking out as he fell to land a glancing blow off Parker's head. By the time Parker got up, the guy had found his feet and charged, giving Parker a taste of his own medicine and slamming him into the car. His brain rattled as though a frying pan had cracked his head, white light flashing across his vision as the air shot from his lungs.

Half a decade of Krav Maga martial arts training kicked in. *Fight dirty.* Parker dug for an eye, and failing that, for the guy's windpipe; he got the latter and the guy backed off. Metal flashed and Parker froze. A butterfly knife glittered as the man lunged at him. Parker stepped back, looking for an escape, then kept moving until he backed into something solid.

Which turned out to be Jane. "Get out of here!" He shoved her away. Green Hat lunged, missed, and tripped over Parker's foot. He dodged back, spotted the shopping bag Jane had dropped. The bag with their latest clue. *Dammit, Jane.* Green Hat wanted it and here it was, along with their old clothes.

The clothes. My shirt. He grabbed the shirt and turned to face his attacker, who now approached with the knife held out. Parker was unarmed, but holding the shirt with both hands like a rope, he did the last thing Green Hat expected. He went right at him. The guy stopped, his knife still. Parker feinted left, dodged the weak stab motion and wrapped the shirt around Green Hat's arm as he twisted and threw his head back full force.

Direct hit to the face. The knife fell free, Parker holding tight to Green Hat's arm as the guy slumped face down on the asphalt, out cold. Parker sucked air greedily.

Jane appeared over his shoulder and nearly got kicked for her trouble. "Hey!" She jumped back. "It's me."

Parker scrambled off his unconscious assailant and fell to his knees. Bile burned in his throat. "I might throw up." Jane backed up even faster. As the world swam back into focus, the urge to retch faded and he managed to get one foot under him. "Is anyone watching us?"

She looked around. "A few people. We should go before security shows up."

"Check his pants."

She stared at him. "What?"

"His pockets." Parker leaned over, rifling the man's shirt. "Wallet, cell phone, something. Maybe we can find out who he is." He hit pay dirt. "Here we go." A cell phone, along with a wad of cash and an inhaler.

"People are coming closer." Jane helped him up, her hand slipping across his neck as he stood. "Your neck is cut."

"No, that's his blood. Come on." Taking his plunder and shirt with him, Parker moved to his car with surprising ease. Must be the adrenaline flowing. When that wore off, his body would come to cash all the checks he'd just written, and it wouldn't be pretty. "You have the bag?" She did. "Then get in. You think it's safe at your home?"

She smirked. "It *is* a castle, remember? I'll call and tell Hugh we're coming."

"Strap in." Driving as fast as he dared, it wasn't until his tires found the expressway on-ramp that he opened it up, bursting off the line in a race for Jane's castle and respite from whoever wanted to kill them. Who they were and *why* this story was worth killing over was what Parker wanted to know.

Right now, however, his best chance to find out was in his glove box – the cell phone and prescription inhaler that could be the key.

Chapter 8

July 8th
Barnbougle Castle
Edinburgh, Scotland

Burning logs cracked and popped, sending tendrils of earthy smoke by Parker's nose while shadows danced across Hugh's beard. The grizzled caretaker had soaked in Jane's tale, silent save an occasional unintelligible mutter.

"This fellow found you at Stirling Castle," Hugh said at last. "How do you think that happened?"

"We don't know," Jane said. "All we can say is sometime between when they left us in the Holy Rude graveyard and when Parker spotted him by the exit, they caught up. Could be someone contacted them."

"Are you sure they didn't just follow you?" Hugh asked.

"I doubt it," Parker said. "I saw their cars at the graveyard, and neither one followed us through Stirling. I pulled off and checked for a tracking device on our way back here. Nothing."

Hugh pointed one gnarled finger at the pilfered cell phone. "What about the text message you showed me on that phone? You can't tell who sent it?"

"I sent it to a government friend," Parker said. "But chances are it's a throwaway phone."

Hugh went to the fireplace and jabbed the logs with a poker. Sparks erupted, floating up the chimney and out of sight. "Not easy getting a pistol these days," he said. "You sure it wasn't an older weapon?"

"I've hunted my whole life. The pistol was a new model."

"These people have resources." Hugh moved from his post in front of the fire and sat down. "The messages you found are involved, I'll wager that."

"I agree," Jane said. "The problem is figuring out what James and Philip were dealing with."

"And who's after us." Parker rubbed a hand over his face, flinching when he hit a growing knot. The damn car bumper had left a mark. Sandpaper scratched his eyes, fatigue doing its best to cloud his mind. "I'm worried about how these goons knew to find us at Stirling Castle."

"You think someone told them where to find us?" Jane twisted her hair again, brunette locks reflecting the firelight. "Who could have known?"

"Let's walk through who knew we were there," Parker said. "Unless your phone is tapped, the information came from someone who either knew our plans or saw us go to Stirling. We need to narrow down who else knew. I'll start." He held up one finger. "My CIA buddy Nick Dean knew we were in Stirling, but not about Stirling Castle. He's the only person I spoke with today."

Jane's strand of hair slowed its endless circle. "I spoke with Evan Ford and Tom Gregan. Evan told me about Stirling, and Tom approved the expenses for our trip."

"Would they have told anyone else?" Parker asked.

"Unlikely."

"What about the paperwork? Who handles that, or has access to the system?"

Jane shrugged. "Anyone with login credentials can view the expense system."

Parker raised an eyebrow. "How many people are you talking about?"

"Anyone in the accounting department. And I suppose a colleague could have overheard my conversation with Evan, or he could have mentioned it to someone." Her hair stopped twisting. "Dozens of people realistically could have known."

Hugh drummed a beat across the tabletop. "Why don't you just ask them, Janie?"

Jane's mouth opened, then closed. She turned to Parker. "What do you think?"

"I think it's a great idea," Parker said. "Start with Evan and Tom, then move on to others. If anybody's story doesn't jibe with what the rest of the staff tells us, we'll at least have a starting point. Can we go in tomorrow?"

"Of course," Jane said. "I wish those two text messages were more specific. All we can tell is they came from an Edinburgh dialing code. Not much to go on."

They'd puzzled over the short messages on the ride home, the only two in the phone's memory.

Targets en route to Stirling Castle. And then the instructions. *Current item is incorrect. Obtain any information targets possess by any means needed.* No names, no locations, nothing other than time stamps indicating the messages had arrived when he and Jane paid the entrance fee at Stirling Castle. Green Hat Man had returned to Stirling Castle and either followed Parker and Jane or saw them as they were leaving.

"Nothing indicates they know about this new message at Stirling." Parker spread his hands on the table, leaning over the patch of leather notepaper. "They found out we had a different message from inside the headstone at Holy Rude, and one of them came back for it."

"Did that man say anything during your fight?" Hugh asked.

"Nothing. When I remembered where the green hat came from, I charged."

"He could have shot us," Jane said. "You didn't know he had a gun."

Parker shrugged. "I didn't think about it. I figured hit him first."

"Best thing in a fight." Hugh slapped Parker's shoulder and looked at Jane. "Lucky for you he did. Now, your government friend is checking the phone messages. What about this?" Hugh picked up the inhaler.

"There's a number on it," Jane said. "Could be a serial number or registration code. Beats me if you can track a person down from that."

"I doubt it," Parker said. "You'd have to get the manufacturer to tell you where it was shipped, and then get the pharmacy to tell you who bought it."

"Could your friend do that?" Hugh asked.

Nick had delivered on harder questions. "Never hurts to ask," he said. Parker composed a text message to Nick, outlining what they had and what he needed to know. He turned back to Hugh. "Any idea about James's message?" He nodded to the scrawled words they had retrieved from Stirling Castle, a single line unlike any of the others.

Hugh leaned toward the leather scrap and read aloud. "*Follow the highest peal of our learned patron. You must look east.*" The caretaker pulled at his beard. "Not much of a sentence."

Parker sent the message to Nick and set his phone down. "About this message. *Peal* and *east* are basically nonsense. Only one part makes sense. How are we supposed to know who their patron was?"

Jane stretched her arms overhead and yawned mightily. "A patron could be a rich person sponsoring the journey, or someone who supported James or Philip even before they started this whole adventure."

"Someone who helped them in the past." Parker spread his hands wide. "We just don't know. I don't see how this helps."

"Don't dismiss it yet," Hugh said. "Is there anything about where you found the messages that could identify James or Philip's last names? Churches keep records; you could check Melrose Abbey and

Holy Rude."

"You're right," Jane said. "The problem is the records are all handwritten. Even with a team it would take forever to dig through them." She patted Hugh's arm. "It's an idea. Right now, we'll take every one we can get."

Parker rubbed his eyes again, pressing gently on the side where he'd been whacked. He was so beat he couldn't think straight. "Maybe a good night's sleep will jog my brain."

"Same here," Jane said. "Tomorrow we can go to my office and dig into this message. My colleagues will be dying to hear about what we've found. They might spot something we missed."

Alarm bells rang in Parker's head. "Are you sure that's a good idea?"

"Why wouldn't it be?"

"We need to be cautious. The only connections we've had with anyone since we found the first message are people from the university and my friend Nick. Someone learned about our plans within hours of us making them. Whoever sent the text messages about us going to Stirling Castle was either from Nick's side or from Edinburgh University."

"It would be smart to take a different car," Hugh said. "In case you were followed. You can take one of ours."

"Thanks. I'll do that," Parker said. "Now, between those two groups of people, where do you suppose the leak came from? An intelligence agent, or someone from the university?"

"None of my colleagues would *ever* do anything like this," Jane said, scowling. "I've known them for years."

"It doesn't have to be someone you know well. You said dozens of people have access to the accounting records. Any of them could figure out where we went next and tell whoever they wanted."

Jane leaned on the table. "I'll talk to Tom and Evan about it tomorrow. Until then, let's get some rest. Parker, you're welcome to stay here."

"We have plenty of space," Hugh said.

Fatigue hung heavy on Parker's entire body, cuts and bruises riding the coattails of exhaustion. "I think I will. I can stop by my place tomorrow morning before we go to your office."

"I'll show you to your room," Hugh said. "A can of antiseptic spray is in order as well. Jane." The magnificent white beard turned her way. "Go to bed, my dear. This problem requires a rested mind to unravel."

She and Hugh shared a swift embrace before Parker followed him upstairs to a bedroom larger than most apartments. The spray stung like hell and everything ached when he laid down, the world fading to dark seconds after Hugh shut off the lights. Funny how warm sheets and a soft pillow worked better than any amount of beer had these past months.

Chapter 9

July 8th

A cigarette holder dangled from the lady's hand, burning red-hot when she inhaled, though the burnt tobacco brought little pleasure. The red tip mirrored her feelings, though the only giveaway was her clenched teeth. Despite the composed look she strived to keep at all times, the man across from her didn't meet her gaze. Both of his hands worked a dingy green hat, twisting it back and forth as he stood.

"You failed." It wasn't a question, and he didn't respond. The lady took her eyes off him, looking out of a window as clouds darted across a half-moon. She paid this man more than enough to complete simple tasks. "Unusual for you. How did it happen?"

More hat-wringing. "He is well-trained in self-defense."

The cigarette brightened, and she blew smoke toward him. "Mr. Jankowski, you must do better than that."

Finally, he met her eyes. "What can I say, ma'am? He caught me solid in the face, knocked me right out. Can't do much when I'm down for the count."

A valid point, and right now she didn't have time to argue. "You should count yourself lucky the police didn't arrest you. Or that Mr. Chase left you with only a headache." Jankowski grumbled, but didn't argue. "Regardless, we must press on. They are moving closer to what I suspect is a wonderful find."

"Any idea what it is, ma'am?"

She stubbed out her cigarette and stood, heels clicking on the floor. "No," she admitted. "However, that does not mean I should not have it. Whatever it may be." She twirled, and the man visibly flinched. "Think about it. What would make you risk your life? This man James – he was running to stay alive. Anything that would make a man do that must be valuable."

"Then you should have it, ma'am."

"Correct." She brushed past him and walked to a desk. A single folder sat on top. "Take this. It is information from my friend at the university. This should tell you how to find them, if not where."

Jankowski looked through the documentation. "Yes, ma'am."

"Anything further I learn will be sent to your phone," she said. "I hope you learned something from this mishap. It surprises me a banker could get the better of you." Jankowski glared. *Good. You should be angry.* "Be more careful this time. Wait until the time is right, preferably without witnesses. Use whatever force is necessary to find the next message from James." A cat jumped onto the desk, and she ran her hand along its back. "Better yet," she said as the cat purred. "Let them find it for you. Dr. White is intelligent. Do not intervene too early. We still do not know everything she does, and it would not be wise on your part to make me lose my prize."

"Of course, ma'am."

"Keep me updated on your progress." She pointed her chin at the door, and Jankowski left. Long after the door clicked shut, she remained standing by the desk, rubbing the cat's ears as she stared outside. *What was Jane White chasing?* The professor had stumbled onto something big. She knew it in her heart. Decades spent collecting the finest prizes of antiquity had given her a sixth sense, a certainty this was legitimate, not some petty prize better left forgotten.

For all she did, a prize she deserved. Look at the good that came from her efforts. Students educated, the community exposed to invaluable knowledge that, without her, would never have come to light. All of it because she shared her wealth. Plus, she appreciated these objects, the scrolls and statues and paintings and relics. Each piece had been given the place of honor it deserved. It didn't matter how many people saw these gifts, or shared in their beauty. The masses had their museums, accessed for a pittance and sustained by the generosity of those like her. With her, in her private showrooms and on her walls, these objects were appreciated.

The lady pressed a call button until her butler appeared. "Ma'am?"

"A martini. And I require more cigarettes." The butler nodded and vanished.

His employer picked up the cat, who purred as she walked around the room. Yes, these walls would do nicely. A pedestal, perhaps, with a spotlight. Depending on what she found, of course. She could already picture it, the new addition to her collection. And who knew, maybe it would be more? There was no certainty in this business. Whatever awaited her at the end, she knew one thing to be certain. She alone could appreciate the prize in the proper manner, and that was why she deserved it.

Chapter 10

July 9th

A needle of light pierced through the darkness, jabbing and prodding Parker from a dreamless slumber until he surfaced above the restful waves, sliding into another day. He opened his eyes to a new world. *Stone walls? That damn window is ten feet tall. Where am I?* All this flashed across his mind before memory's faulty circuits warmed up. *Philip's trail. The man in the green hat. I'm in Jane's castle.*

He grabbed his phone. Eight in the morning. Time to get moving if he wanted to run home before heading to Jane's office. He'd slept like a baby and had needed it. As his feet hit the floor, the memory of his fight arrived in the form of pain. Head, back, one knee, both hands. Everything hurt, in any number of ways. Jolting pain here, a throbbing there, all on top of the usual aches from half a lifetime of playing football. A few pops and cracks he knew like old friends. Everything else was new and wholly unwelcome.

Fighting is a young man's game. Now all he had to do was remember it. Running. That he could do. How did the saying go? You live longer if you don't stay for every scrap. As he struggled to get upright, accented voices filtered into his room, Jane and Hugh down near the fireplace. A warm fire sounded great right now, almost as nice as a hot shower at his place. And if he played his cards right, Hugh might show him the hidden passages before he left. Beaten body or not, that wasn't a sight to be missed.

"Good morning." Parker hobbled straight for the fire. "Is that coffee I smell?"

"It is," Hugh said, rearranging the burning logs. "Help yourself. I hope you found the accommodations to your liking."

"Fantastic." Parker filled a mug and joined Jane at the table. She folded her hands around her cup, a wisp of a smile stuck on her lips. "I slept like the dead."

"You look like the dead," Jane said. "That's going to be a nice bruise on your face."

His head throbbed, but damned if he'd admit it. "I'm fine. What time do you go to the office?"

"When the spirit moves me," she said. "I'm normally in by nine."

"Then I should get moving. The sooner we figure out what James was telling Philip, the better chance we have of never seeing any goons again." Parker gulped coffee and burned his tongue. "Before I leave, I have to ask a favor." He said this last part to Hugh, who set the poker down and crossed his arms.

"What would that be, my young friend?"

"Jane tells me you have secret passages here. I'd love to see them."

"They won't be secret for long if she keeps telling everyone." Hugh fixed Jane with a mock frown. "Miss White?"

"We can let him in on it," she said. "In truth, they're quite hard to spot unless you know what to look for."

"Like all things well hidden," Parker said. "In the dark or in plain sight."

"More true than you realize," Hugh said. "Come over here." Parker followed him to a spot halfway between the fireplace and an arched entranceway. "What do you see?"

"A stone wall." Decorative carvings framed the hearth on one side, with a doorway on the other. "I don't see anything." Hugh stepped aside, and Parker squinted harder. "Wait a second. What is that, a medallion?" He touched a metal disc on the wall; a flowing *X* was carved into the circle.

"It's Saint Andrew's Cross," Hugh said.

Jane spoke from the table. "Saint Andrew is the patron saint of Scotland. In the ninth century Oengus II was king of the Picts, the group later known as Scots. His army fought a battle against the Angles, who eventually helped form England. According to legend, Oengus and his army were heavily outnumbered, so he prayed to Saint Andrew and promised to make him the patron saint of Scotland if they defeated the English. Supposedly he saw an X-shaped cross in the clouds after winning the battle; he kept his word."

Hugh picked up the tale. "Now the saltire, or Saint Andrew's Cross, is on the Scottish flag. It is also the type of cross on which the saint was crucified."

"Interesting," Parker said, and he meant it. "Why do you have one on the wall?"

"There are four medallions," Hugh said. "One on each door of the hidden passageways."

Parker took a step back. Other than the medallion, nothing about this section of wall stood out. "Where's the doorway?"

"The stones stick out enough to shadow the opening," Jane said. "Hugh, show him."

Hugh picked up a flashlight from the fireplace mantel. "This is one upper corner." Illuminating a point on the wall slightly above Parker's head, he motioned for Parker to come closer. "Look between these two stones. Do you see it now?"

"I do." A tiny fissure ran between the stones, all of which managed to follow a relatively straight line despite their uneven edges. "Impressive," Parker said as Hugh ran his light around the frame, outlining where it touched the floor on either side. "How do you open it?"

"This is the best part," Hugh said. "I'll tell you the medallion is involved. Care to guess how?"

Parker pushed and prodded the metal symbol to no avail. "I give up."

"You were close." Hugh reached out and twisted it. "That's all it takes." Something clicked, and a second later the door slid back on silent hinges.

"How's it do that? I didn't hear anything."

"Counterweights and hinges," Hugh said. "When I came here as a young man, the damn thing made more noise than a rocket. Jane's father installed new materials so it makes nary a peep."

"Can I go inside?" Precious little light penetrated the dark void. "I can't see anything."

"There's a light switch," Jane said. "Along with a button to close the door. But there's something you should know before you go to the basement."

He turned to find her standing by the table, hands still folded around her coffee mug. "You have booby traps in there?"

"I don't mean this passage. It's about the message from Stirling Castle."

That stopped him. "What about it?" Jane merely grinned. "You know what James was talking about."

"I didn't unravel it. Hugh did."

"When?"

"Last night," Hugh said. The secret door swung shut without a sound. "It occurred to me before I fell asleep. What the message really meant."

Neither of his hosts spoke, both looking at him with those faint, semi-British smiles. "What does it mean?"

Jane broke first. "Go on, Hugh. No reason to keep him in suspense."

Hugh touched his beard. "One word struck me as odd. A word with different meanings, including one I never considered until I tended the fire last night before bed." He pointed to the poker. "That fell over after I set it down. Right there where you're standing, Parker. When I picked it up, what was I looking at?"

Parker turned to find the formerly mysterious medallion. "This design."

"Correct," Hugh said. "Saint Andrew's Cross. Any ideas?"

"None at all," Parker said. "As is often the case."

"Saint Andrew," the caretaker said. "The *patron* saint of Scotland."

Parker nearly spit his coffee out. "James wasn't talking about someone funding his journey. He meant their religious patron."

"As in a *protector*," Jane said. "He's talking about Scotland's cherished saint."

Parker furrowed his brow. "How can you be sure? Andrew isn't the only saint."

"I'm reasonably certain in this case," Jane said. "One, James is most likely Scottish, which means Philip is too. The first saint in their minds is Andrew. Second, he describes the patron as *learned*." Here Parker raised an eyebrow. "That can only mean one thing here. The University of St. Andrews."

Hard to argue with the logic. "How long has it been around?"

"Since the fifteenth century. Well before James or Philip were born."

His heart beat a little faster. "Nicely done, Hugh."

"It was mostly luck." Hugh nodded to Jane. "She uncovered everything else."

Parker waited, then cleared his throat. "Willing to share it?"

Jane laughed. "Take the message piece by piece." Pointing to the leather scrap on their oversized table, she read again. "We have an idea of the end portion, but what about the beginning? *'Follow the highest peal'* and *'You must look east'* aren't clear taken alone. However, if we're correct about St. Andrew, it makes sense if you know details about the university."

Parker walked over. "Such as?"

"Landmarks and structures." She pointed to one word. "Start with *peal.* The sound a bell makes, and there are two bells on campus, both chapels. St. Salvator's and St. Leonard's."

"Is one at the eastern end?"

"I don't believe so," Jane said. "I'll verify that when I get to my office. St. Salvator's is by far the most well-known chapel. It's the tallest, and most well-attended. When anyone talks about a chapel at the university, St. Salvator's comes to mind. This would have been true three hundred years ago."

"I can work with that," Parker said. "If Salvator's isn't on the eastern side of campus, why tell Philip to look in that direction?"

"The chapel has always been open to the public. James would have had little trouble accessing the building. My guess is he's pointing us to the bell tower's eastern side."

Ignoring his rising pulse, Parker worried his lip. "It seems convenient. Maybe too convenient."

"I could be wrong, of course, but it's all we have to go on."

"Have faith," Hugh said. "A little belief won't hurt you."

"It's too much faith that worries me." Parker drained his coffee mug. "Your logic is sound." His hand went out, and Jane slapped him five. "One question. Do you think any of these clues James left behind might be misdirection? He had people trying to catch him and get whatever it is he was so keen to keep away from them. Don't you think he may have led these people on a wild goose chase?"

"I doubt it," Jane said. "His messages make it sound like what he's carrying is easily portable, and I get the sense these stops are part evasive, part security. Every place he left a clue was a chance to lie low, collect himself or get a night's rest. He had to sleep, and as long as those chasing him didn't suspect he was leaving messages behind, he could take an evening here and there and not worry if someone saw him."

"His goal was to deliver the final message to Philip," Hugh said. "Which he didn't do. That failure is what created this trail for you and Jane to follow."

"If he wanted to keep people off balance, this was a good way to do it," Parker said. "We'll never know." He turned to Jane. "When can we go to your office? We're not the only ones reconstructing this trail."

"Let me get my things together and we can leave," Jane said. "Do you want to stop by your place?"

"Heading there now. I'll meet you at your office." He offered his hand to Hugh and got a handshake of iron in return. "Thanks for the hospitality."

"Watch your back, Parker. Jane and I are counting on you."

"I'm on it." With a hand on the front door, he turned back. "How far is St. Andrews from here?"

"A ninety-minute drive," Jane said. "No reason we can't go there today."

"Great. Don't forget to bring one of your estate cars," he said. "Let's leave mine at your office, just in case those goons hope to follow it again."

Jane nodded, and he jumped into his Mustang and flew across town, stopping at his flat just long enough to shower and change clothes. Two extra-strength painkillers dulled the assorted aches enough to clear his head. Ten minutes and only one questionable yellow stoplight decision later, he parked outside the university and found Jane's office without any false turns. Her door was propped open, but before he walked in a man's voice caught his ear. Parker stopped in the entranceway, trying to connect a face to the words.

"Do you still have the container?"

A younger man's voice, one he'd heard before. *Evan Ford.* The graduate assistant. Hopefully Jane hadn't told him about St. Andrews yet. As far as Parker was concerned, everybody was a suspect in their hunt to find the leak. He peered around the corner to get a view of her office.

"It's on the examination table," Jane said. "Would you check it out for me? There's probably not much to find other than rust."

"Of course," Evan said. He turned to leave, folding a pair of glasses into his shirt pocket. "If you'll be here all day, I'll bring the results over when I'm finished."

Parker stepped directly into the younger man's path. "Oh, excuse me. Good morning."

The slender man bounced off Parker, quickly smoothing his well-pressed shirt with both hands as he studied the larger man. Light shined off a bald spot no hair artistry could conceal. "Good morning, Mr. Chase." Evan reached out and pumped his hand, doing little to help the pain emanating from each bruised knuckle. "I understand you and Jane made progress with your search." Evan's head tilted to one side, his eyes narrow as he adjusted his glasses. "Are you okay, Mr. Chase? Looks like you had a fall."

"A little accident. Nothing to worry about." He dropped Evan's hand and stepped aside. "Call me Parker. The whole mister thing makes me feel old."

"Understood," Evan said. "Jane, I'll be back with those results." With that, he bolted from the room, humming as he went.

"Before you ask," Jane said, holding up a hand. "No, I didn't tell him we discovered where the next message points. I barely gave him time to look at it. Now be honest with me." She stepped around him and checked the hall before continuing. "Does Evan Ford look like the kind of person who is mixed up with gun-toting gangsters?"

"Appearances can be deceiving. Yes, he looks like a meek academic, but that means nothing. Some of the toughest guys I've ever met look like wimps. As to whether or not he could be selling us out, same answer. For all we know Evan Ford is a cold-blooded killer." Parker's hands went up. "There's no way to tell. Better to be safe and suspect everyone."

"It's hard to picture Evan doing anything to hurt me."

"Let's hope you're right." A glowing computer screen caught his eye. "So, what can you tell me about St. Salvator's?"

"The chapel has one bell tower, here." She twisted the monitor toward him to display a ground-level snapshot of the tower, square and harsh in soft sunlight, rising to a conical point four stories above the road. "There are six bells in the tower, which is used regularly."

Stained glass of brilliant colors cut the severe gothic architecture, producing a unique beauty that spoke across centuries. "Can we get inside the bell tower?" Parker asked.

"The chapel is open to the public. As for the bell tower, I'm not sure. I suggest we start on the ground and work our way up. If we run into restricted areas, we can deal with that."

"I like the way you think. Is there anything special about the east side of the bell tower? Carvings, inscriptions maybe?" Jane shook her head. "Good," Parker said. "If there were, I think it would have been harder for James to leave a clue. A plain wall is better for us."

"Today it would be hard for someone to access the tower without staff noticing," Jane said. "Three hundred years ago James could have slipped in at night past any guards or priests who happened to be there. Or for all we know he had help on the inside. Given how well he's managed to sneak in and out of places so far, I'm not worried about this trip being all for nothing."

"Here's hoping he knew how to trespass."

A knock sounded at Jane's door. "Come in," she said. Parker closed the webpage on St. Salvator's. "Good morning, Tom." Jane flipped a notepad over. "How are you?"

"Excellent, thank you." Parker turned to see Tom Gregan approaching, a megawatt smile leading the way. "We have a special guest visiting today, and I wanted to introduce her to our staff." Tom stepped aside to reveal a woman who apparently hadn't eaten for weeks. Probably because she spent all her money on diamonds. "This is Grace Astor."

At the mention of her name, Jane randomly grabbed at the papers strewn across her workspace and disorganized them even further. "Ms. Astor, welcome. I didn't know you were coming or I would have tidied up."

"A woman at work is a beautiful thing." Grace marched past Tom, whose shining leather shoes clicked as he jumped aside. "I trust you have everything you need?"

"Yes, no small thanks to you. I cannot begin to tell you how much the university appreciates your generosity."

"Work such as yours is thanks enough." Grace turned to Parker, and he nearly took a step back. "I don't believe I've met you yet." She came straight for him, this time forcing Jane to clear out of her way. "Are you a new member of the department?" She stopped close enough to let Parker know she'd heard of personal space and didn't think other people had any.

"No, ma'am. I'm a friend of Dr. White's."

"A friend, come all the way from America?" Her gaze ran over Parker's frame. Lips glossed in brilliant red pursed. "You should cut your hair, young man. Far too handsome a face to hide under those overgrown locks. And don't call me ma'am. It's insulting."

Heat touched his cheeks; one hand froze halfway to his hair tie. "My apologies, Ms. Astor."

"None needed." She studied him a second longer before turning back to Jane. "Tom tells me you have a new project." Refracted light danced across the walls when she leaned over the assorted paperwork and artifacts, a beautiful, unimaginably expensive light show glittering and flashing from her jewelry. "All from a dead man's pocket, isn't it?"

"I found a message sewn into a shirt. The shirt's previous owner was found behind a wall in Craigmillar Castle. We think he was tortured before he died."

"No doubt in an attempt to locate this letter," Grace said. "Where do you keep your ashtray?" Before anyone could object, Grace Astor whipped out a silver cigarette case. "And a lighter, please."

She may as well have asked Jane where she kept her mustard gas. "*Ashtray?* I'm afraid you can't smoke in here, Ms. Astor. University policy."

Grace Astor was not impressed. "I don't work here, Dr. White. I'm sure it's acceptable for visitors to smoke."

Tom Gregan's neck muscles worked overtime. "Ms. Astor, I'm terribly sorry, but if you smoke in here the fire alarms will activate."

The cigarette remained between her fingers. Nobody moved until Grace Astor let out a soft sigh. "In that case, I need some fresh air. Tom, you will escort me to my car."

"Of course." The red creeping up Tom's neck vanished. "Right this way."

"Not yet." She turned to Jane. "What has happened since you found the letter? Have you made progress?"

With everyone's threat level backed off from peak smoking worry, Jane outlined their efforts so far, leaving out any parts about armed men, St. Salvator's Chapel or St. Andrews. "I haven't had a chance to research the most recent information. Once we do, I will pass on an update."

"Wonderful," Grace said. "A mystery sprung from a dead man, with no indication as to the end result. Quite the fortunate turn when the corpse turned up."

"Not for James," Parker said, softly enough that only Jane could hear.

"It certainly is," Jane said, fighting a grin. "It's always a pleasure to see you."

"Keep Evan apprised of your progress," Grace called over her shoulder as she swept toward the door. "I speak with him regularly. Good luck, Jane." She disappeared, and Tom scurried along behind her.

It was as though a storm had blown through. Grace Astor's reach certainly extended far beyond her arm's length.

"That is one unique woman." The meeting couldn't have lasted more than five minutes, yet Ms. Astor had crammed more personality into the brief exchange than should be possible. "She's always that way?"

"That was nothing." Jane shut the door. "She's something. Rich, powerful, borderline nutty, to name a few."

"Eccentric," Parker said. "Rich people aren't crazy, they're eccentric. One perk of having money."

"Grace Astor is the largest university donor, individual or corporate, the bulk of which goes to historical research." Jane flipped her laptop open. "No husband or kids. Speaking of which." Jane winked at him. "Grace liked the looks of you. If you cut those overgrown locks, of course."

Again, a hand went to his hair. "It's not that bad." He touched the ends of his pitiful ponytail. "Is it?"

"Very European. Not sure the whole man-bun look is your style, but who am I to judge?"

"I don't have a man-bun." That settled it – he was cutting this damn thing off. As soon as they found whatever James was hiding. "Leave my hair out of this, if you don't mind. Speaking of which, nice work with the misdirection. No reason to give away all our information, even to a big donor."

"To be honest, I'm not *entirely* certain the clue points to St. Salvator's. Better if we confirm it first before sharing."

"Agreed. That goes for everyone around here, not just Grace. Seems she has someone keeping her updated about what we're doing."

"Which is why I didn't mention the gunmen." Jane tapped the keyboard as she spoke. "You saw how excited she got about everything. Add an element of danger to the mix and there would be no stopping her." She grabbed a backpack from the floor and hefted it over one shoulder. "I searched several additional locations which generally fit the clue we found. If anyone's monitoring my computer, they'll have to sort through everything to figure out where we went, and by that time we'll at least be at St. Salvator's, if not further along."

"Good thinking. You brought a different car?"

"One of our estate vehicles," she said. "Like you suggested. Nothing fancy, but Hugh promised the engine is second to none. Four-wheel drive, too."

"I like it. Let's go."

He hadn't made it two steps before the door flew open and Evan Ford burst in, clutching a stack of books. "I brought these along in case you needed to research Stirling Castle or the town in any more depth. I confess, even though I grew up near the area, my knowledge of Stirling is limited."

"Thanks," Jane said. "Everything you told me before was a big help."

Evan studied her desk as he replied. "Did you ever find anything? Another message from the dead man? James, I think his name was."

"Yes, it was. And I'm not certain." Jane glanced over at Parker. "I haven't had a chance to fully review everything."

"I'd be delighted to help."

Jane reached out and patted his narrow shoulder. "You'll be the first person I call."

"We're not entirely in the dark," Parker said. "Jane believes we may have to return to Stirling Castle. It could be James hid another message in or near the graveyard."

Evan perked up. "Is that so? Why the graveyard?"

"Call it a hunch," Jane said. "It's best if we go back and have a look around."

"James seems to like graveyards," Evan said. "Is there any research I can do?"

"Not right now. If we find anything else, I'll let you know."

"Excellent," Evan said. "You'll be going along, Parker?"

He nodded. "It's not every day an expert like Jane gives tours of Scotland."

"I'm hardly an expert." She tapped the books Evan had brought. "Thanks again for your help. We'd better get on the road."

"I'll be in the office all day," Evan said as he followed them out of her office. "Don't hesitate to call."

Jane assured him they wouldn't, and as Evan disappeared down the hallway, Parker watched until he turned a corner. "Evan really wanted to help us."

"He's a good student. Enthusiastic, a bit aimless with his studies, but very bright." She led Parker to a different lot than where he'd parked; this one was around back, covered in a blanket of shade cast by towering trees. "Evan may sound like a lost academic, but he's far from it. Nice bit about the graveyard. Quick on your feet."

Lights flashed on a Mercedes sedan when Jane hit her keys. "That's your extra car?" Parker asked.

"One of them. It belongs to my parents," she said quickly.

"How many of these are at your castle?"

"Don't concern yourself with our vehicle situation. Get in."

He slid into the passenger seat. "About the graveyard, I figured it made sense. Let Evan connect the dots and it's more believable. If it turns out he's the one passing on our whereabouts, at least they'll head in the wrong direction."

"St. Andrew's is over an hour's drive from Stirling," Jane said. "By the time they figure out we're not there, we'll have found James's next message and be on our way."

Parker reached over, and she slapped his palm. "I like your attitude."

Jane goosed it as they pulled onto the main road, sending Parker back in his seat and chirping the tires. "Told you this girl has enough power for us."

Parker's pocket buzzed. "It's Nick." He connected the call on speaker. "Good morning. My friend Jane is in the car."

"It's the middle of the night here." Nick's voice filled the cozy vehicle. "I got a lead on your vehicle tags. The car is a rental out of Edinburgh, paid for with a credit card belonging to one Benjamin Young."

"Did you find anything on this guy?"

"Mr. Young is in his mid-forties, and his listed address is in the city."

"Does he have a criminal record?"

"No. Two details about the man jumped out at me. His address is in a commercial complex, and his apartment is currently vacant. The prior tenant was a bakery that relocated last year, and the surrounding units are all businesses. The place doesn't have any residential units." Parker frowned at Jane before Nick continued. "The second detail is more interesting. According to national insurance number records, which are like our social security numbers, the Benjamin Young who rented this car died thirty-nine years ago at age four."

"He used a fake identity," Parker said. "Any luck tracing it?"

"I didn't have any success with the rental agency or credit card company. As long as you have a national insurance number and pay your bills, this company doesn't ask questions."

"Then we're back at the beginning," Jane said.

"Not quite," Nick said. "Ask me about the inhaler." They asked in unison. "Obtaining a prescription for anything isn't easy to do with a fake identity. That's why I think this guy used his real name to get it. I traced the serial number on his albuterol back to the issuing pharmacy. It was prescribed for a Christopher Jankowski."

"Find anything out about him?" Parker asked.

"He was a Glasgow police officer for over a decade, until he resigned after an arrest he made put someone in the hospital. My guess is his resignation had something to do with the half-million-pound settlement the department paid out. Next, he worked at a private security firm, guarding rich people's homes and serving as a bodyguard. I couldn't get his client list, but five years ago he quit that private security gig and became self-employed. He now reports making over a hundred thousand pounds per year, and he lives in Edinburgh."

"No idea who he works for?" Parker asked.

"None. Given his steady income my guess is he's been working for the same employer since he went out on his own. I asked a friend to see what he can turn up." Nick took a deep breath. "Stay away from him. This guy is not worried about hurting people."

"You know where he lives," Parker said.

"I do, and I'm not sharing. There's a question you need to ask."

Jane beat him to it. "Why is a private security man after us?"

"Bingo," Nick said. "Your search caught his employers' attention. Why?"

"We don't even know what we're searching for," Parker said. "None of the letters says what James was carrying around, only that people are after him for it, but he never mentions who they are."

"Either Jankowski's employer knows what's waiting at the end of your search, or they think it's worth following you to find it." Nick took a deep breath. "Consider the facts, Parker. You are a U.S. citizen in a country you don't know. Neither of you are trained to handle this."

"We have you to help us."

"I'm in America," Nick said. "I have a full-time job, which doesn't include saving your neck. That being said," and here Parker detected a tinge of excitement in Nick's words, "I can't tell you what to do. Not that you or Erika ever listened anyway."

Parker's chest dropped. He and Erika had done risky things in the past. Done them one too many times. He turned to Jane. "Nick's right. We shouldn't be doing this. It's dangerous." Certainly not with Jane, a scholar like Erika. Encouraging her to chase this fragmented puzzle was reckless, and he should know better. This could get them killed.

"What would Erika say?" Jane asked. Her question hit him hard. "Erika wasn't afraid. She loved her work, lived for it, and if she had a chance like this, she'd take it." Jane's hands grew white on the wheel. "Tell me I'm wrong."

Sunlight sliced through the scattered clouds above and warmed Parker's face. "I can't." Simple as that, if he wanted to be honest. Erika would have dived into this headfirst. "Nick, we aren't stopping now."

"I thought you'd say that," Nick said. "Okay, I'll stop preaching. As an agent of the U.S. government, I can't aid you in potentially criminal activities. But I'm on a coffee break right now, so let's chat. I have friends in Scotland who can help. One's in Edinburgh, another in Glasgow. If you need anything, call me."

"I'll keep that in mind," Parker said.

"Now, I have to get back to work. Don't do anything stupid, and don't go looking for Christopher Jankowski by yourself. The guy is trouble. Oh, I almost forgot. This could be nothing, but when I told my friend why I was calling, he mentioned something."

"You told him what we're doing?"

"Only that you found an old message on a dead guy and are destroying all kinds of Scottish heritage. Is that a problem?"

"Funny."

"I never joke," Nick deadpanned. "My friend mentioned an investigation he's been part of for the past few years, one revolving around stolen artifacts purchased for serious money. There's a large market for these things all across Europe, including Scotland."

"It's a big business," Jane said. "My colleagues have issues with sites being looted and museums robbed. Some private collectors pay top dollar for rare artifacts."

"Collectors who can afford to hire hard men to solve their problems," Nick said. "Don't take these people lightly."

Parker promised they wouldn't, and Jane waited until he clicked off before speaking. "This help Nick mentioned. Is he talking about guns?" Parker nodded. "Do you really know how to use a gun?"

"I'm American, remember? They teach us that stuff in gym class." Her jaw dropped. "I'm kidding. I hunted growing up. I've used them my entire life."

"Guns frighten me."

"They should. If you have a gun, you should know what you're doing. And always hope you don't need to use it."

"Let's get in and out of St. Salvator's before anybody realizes we're here." Jane patted his leg. "You're a smart guy. We can solve this without weapons."

"Flattery will get you everywhere," he said. "But I agree."

They spent the rest of the trip discussing St. Salvator's, Parker mostly listening while Jane described the geography and setup. Based on her summary, they should be able to gain access to most any part of the chapel, though as the storied, ancient campus came into view, the only certain thing was that they had a lot of ground to cover with just these centuries-old clues as their guide.

Gothic buildings lined the modern paved streets; the sidewalks were bustling with students. Amazing, considering St. Andrews University had stood since roughly 1410. Despite the sunshine, many of the older buildings maintained an aura of stoic, shadowy solitude as they passed, dominated by stained glass, wrought iron and sharp angles. The people who built this place had viewed education as a solemn pursuit, meant to be respected and appreciated.

"You can see the tower from here." Jane indicated a square structure rising above the dark rooftops, topped with what resembled a stone wizard's hat. Tall, narrow openings revealed a number of bells. "Hopefully we don't have to climb that high. Chances are it's restricted up there."

"I don't see any guardrails." Parker shaded his eyes, leaning out the window to get a better view. "You fall from there, it won't be pretty."

In a minor miracle, Jane found an open parking spot along the street. They left the car and fell into step with the stream of pedestrians young and old moving about campus before Jane led them off the main drag and along a crenellated wall. Parker ran his fingers over its uneven stones and rough mortar. "I say we stick together."

"Agreed," Jane said. "Act like tourists. Look around, be curious, try not to break anything."

"And keep an eye open for trouble." They entered St. Salvator's under the watchful gaze of an unnamed saint in a stained-glass window. Cool air raised the hair on his neck, the chapel's interior stretching out ahead. "I've never seen a church set up like this."

Pews rose like stadium seats along each wall, facing each other, which forced all the parishioners to stare at their fellow worshippers while the service went on far down the aisle at a marble altar with paintings in front of and behind it.

"This isn't unusual for the time period," Jane said. "Come on, the tower is this way." They squeezed through a tiny side door exit. Warm wind met them as they stepped into an open quad boasting an immense area of grass. Pillars lined the walkway.

"Can you only get into the tower from outside?"

"The stairs are behind the organ," Jane said. "This is quicker than going through the chapel, and fewer people will notice us. There's a back door that leads to the tower over here."

They entered a room overrun with tidy rows of simple wooden chairs, hymnals laid out on each. "What is this?" he asked, dodging around a bright yellow SLIPPING HAZARD sign standing guard over a mop bucket and safety cone.

"The door should be right here." She produced a piece of paper with her handwritten notes. "This one." She indicated a door overlaid with iron strips, the kind of door put up to keep people out. "This is how you get inside the tower." It opened under her touch. Not much good for keeping people out if you didn't lock it, Parker mused.

"Are we allowed in here?"

"The door's unlocked. If they didn't want people inside, they'd lock it," Jane said. "Watch your head."

Things got low and narrow in a hurry. Steps twisted up and

around, lit by thin strips of sunlight falling through arrow slits. "I wasn't a boy scout, but the sun rises in the east so I think we're on the east side of the tower."

"I knew Erika kept you around for a reason." Jane stopped in her tracks. "You take one side and I'll take the other. Let me do the talking if anyone shows up. I'll say I couldn't find the bathroom."

Parker and Jane inspected the stone walls with one ear open for intruders. Thick chunks of rock carved in roughly straight lines offered little insight into anything other than their ability to block any heat from getting inside. Parker did his searching with a beam of sunlight on his back, the only respite from the chill. "Living in a place like this would be awful," he said.

"Only society's intellectual members stayed in such luxurious accommodations." Jane sneezed. "Sorry about that. Those men, and it was almost all men, who spent years cramped in these places are the reason learning eventually triumphed over ignorance and conflict. The monks who copied books helped spread knowledge. Without them our Dark Ages would have lasted much longer and the Renaissance might never have happened."

"At least copying manuscripts kept them moving. Better than sitting and freezing."

Jane stood from her crouch. "That's it for the east side on this level. Time to move up."

"Do you think we should start at the top and work our way down?" Parker asked. "James's message said *'the highest peal'*."

"He could be referencing the bell tower's height. It's the tallest tower. Better to work our way up and be thorough, don't you think?"

"The longer we search, the greater the chances of someone showing up."

"Then stop talking. We'll be at the top soon enough." Jane disappeared up the curving stone steps. Parker followed, always a few steps behind given the staircase was scarcely wide enough for two people. They inspected the second and third eastern-side steps in silence, finding nothing more than dust.

"It doesn't look like these stones have ever been touched." Parker tugged on the metal guiderail. "Other than putting plastic shields over the windows, it could be the same as when James came here."

"*If* James came here. And yes, I agree. Whatever James may have left behind is more likely to still be here."

An open door waited around the next curve. "Are those ropes hanging in there?" Parker nudged Jane aside to stick his head into the room. A half-dozen ropes dangled from above, though even with his neck craned fully back he couldn't tell what waited at the other end.

"Connected to the bells," Jane said. "The bell ringers use ropes to move them."

Made sense. "It's a long way up."

"A few more stories," Jane said. "It's dark up there so it looks farther. The bells are so big they block most of the sunlight."

They moved up another level. Parker paused to look out of one of the narrow windows. St. Andrew's campus spread out on all sides far below him; miniature people strolled busily about. He resumed his climb and then, distracted, smacked into Jane when she stopped without warning.

"Whoa – you okay?" he said, putting a hand on the stone wall for balance.

"I'm fine." She sighed. "Actually, there's something I wanted to ask." Kneeling on a step several feet above him, she didn't turn to face him. "I understand if you don't want to answer."

His chest went tight, the air suddenly cooler. "What's on your mind?"

"It's about Erika." Now she turned around, looking down from her perch. Wind whistled through invisible cracks in the walls. "I couldn't attend her funeral, and I never got a chance to ask anyone."

"About what happened," he said. Jane nodded. "Fair question. I couldn't talk about it. Not for the reasons you'd expect." She waited, watching him. Letting him talk when he was ready. "It's hard to believe. You'll think I'm nuts."

Still she didn't speak. Parker took a deep breath. *Where to start?* Outside of the police, he'd never really talked about this with anyone. Nick, once, but only over the phone. "Everyone thinks her death was an accident, but it wasn't. Erika was murdered." Jane gasped. "And I know who did it." He raised a hand, warding off the inevitable question. "I can't prove it, but I'm positive the man who killed her lives in London and works for the Queen." A look of confusion flashed across Jane's face. "It only gets stranger from there."

"You wouldn't make that up, so I believe you."

"The man who killed Erika put an explosive device in my car. The police found traces of accelerant, and the materials were military grade. The official explanation I got was that a terrorist group wanted to scare off tourists, so they picked our car at random." His voice took the same hard edge he always imagined it would. "That's impossible."

"Why?"

"Because we had been helping the only terrorists in Ireland who could do that."

"You're talking about the Irish Republican Army."

"I am. Erika accidentally got us in the middle of a situation with the British government on one side and the IRA on the other. Turns out the supposed bad guys weren't so bad after all, and when everything settled down, I believe someone in the government wanted payback."

"If you know this, why can't they be arrested?"

His teeth ground together. "The man and his group are protected. I can't touch them."

"What do you mean, protected?"

His voice echoed off the walls. "Erika was someone who got in the way and had to be dealt with. By sheer luck, I ended up with third-degree burns while my fiancée got a casket and headstone."

Jane's eyes went wide. "Did you say fiancée?"

He looked up. "Erika and I got engaged the day before she died."

Jane walked down and gently touched his arm. "I am so sorry."

It was nice of her to say that, Parker thought, nicer still that that was all she said. The last thing he wanted was a rambling monologue. "I appreciate it. Though you know if Erika were here right now, she'd tell us to get moving."

Jane smiled, her eyes wet. "She would. I loved that about her." Jane was silent for a few moments. After they'd searched for a bit longer, she spoke again. "How did Erika get the government's attention?"

"I'll tell you sometime. Promise." Jane seemed to accept this, and before he realized how far they'd gone, the staircase ran out of stairs.

"This leads to the bells."

"How do you know that?" Parker asked.

"The door label." Jane smirked, stepping aside to reveal a metal plaque.

Parker slid past her and pushed the door open. "Lots of trusting people here. Don't they lock any doors?"

"Let's hope not." Jane darted ahead, holding her cell phone aloft for light. "Here it is." She flicked a switch, and weak light dribbled down the walls. "What's that noise?"

Parker turned one ear toward her. "You mean the swishing sound?"

"Yes." Jane pointed to a wall standing alone in the room's center. "It's coming from behind there." With her phone light leading the way, Jane peered around one edge before jumping back into Parker's chest. "It's a swinging pendulum."

Behind the wall a pendulum as tall as a man whipped back and forth, slicing the air every second. "Must be for the clock on this tower." A circuit of the room revealed one major problem. "We're out of doors," he said. "Only one way up from here."

A set of wooden stairs led into the ceiling. "Those are the steepest stairs I've ever seen." Jane grabbed each of the handrails and gave them a good shake. "Seems solid."

"They wouldn't want bell ringers breaking their necks," Parker said. "Come on." Without waiting for her approval, he vaulted up the stairs two at a time, heading into darkness. What he found at the top was not encouraging. "More steps up here."

"Come back down. Let's search here before we move up." This part of the tower didn't have actual floors, only landings, barely large enough for two people. The stone walls looked original, but the wooden stairs and boards at each landing had been added. No way they'd been around when James was alive. "This wood isn't three hundred years old. Listen to it." He stamped on one board, producing barely a thud even in the tight quarters. "This is recent. No squeaky floors here."

After both landings and a narrow walkway revealed nothing, Jane pointed to the dark ceiling overhead, really a floor hiding the tower's main attraction. "Last stop. We're running out of options."

"Unless we missed it," Parker said, though he didn't believe it. They'd scoured every inch of these walls and found nothing remotely resembling a message. If James had left anything behind, it waited in the bell tower. Ascending one more staircase, they entered the bell chamber. Parker couldn't see five feet in the gloom. "Hold on."

Jane waited on the ladder while he skirted the bells and their casings, reaching for the closest window and sliding the wooden slats open. Warm light arced across the room, cut by thin black lines every few feet. The distant sound of traffic moving and horns honking filled his ears.

"Someone could see those open," Jane said. "Start searching." Ignoring the huge instruments in the room's center, she crouched down and inspected the wall. Parker studied the bells for a moment, piecing together what he'd seen below with the contraption up here. What looked like wagon wheels stood on either side of each bell; ropes ran along each wheel's circumference, with both ends disappearing into the floor. Neat concept. A bell ringer took one side of the rope, waited while his partner pulled on the opposing end to get the bell moving, and then they pulled, using the bell's massive weight to keep the momentum going.

"See anything?" Jane asked.

"Not yet." Sunlight dappled his fingers and glistened on dust motes dancing on a cross-breeze cutting through the room. Next to him, Jane's hair caught the light and flashed a golden hue. The hair color of a girl he used to know, and that image stopped him cold.

"When Erika and I were in Ireland," he began, not looking at Jane, "we got involved with the IRA based on a letter one of her former classmates found."

Jane stopped moving. "Do I know her?"

"No. She was an art historian. She found a letter from Queen Anne hidden in a painting."

Jane let the past tense slip by. "How did it involve the IRA?"

"It told a story about them and the government. It was the government's people who killed Erika. The IRA guys were the good ones as far as I'm concerned."

Now Jane stood, not turning to face him, but searching along the window's edge. "Was the letter that important?"

Parker barked a bitter laugh. "To some people. Other people died because of it." A man he'd become fast friends with had been killed trying to protect his country. And the other side suffered too, losing a soldier who'd tried to stop Parker at each turn, only to lose everything in a way no one could have imagined. And for what? A piece of paper and ultimately meaningless words. Meaningless because those in power didn't want to read them, truth or not. "It was all horseshit."

When he didn't resume speaking, Jane tapped a brick in front of her face. "You should see this."

Dark anger simmered inside him, the despair six months of boozing had failed to extinguish. "What is it?"

"It's a message."

He nearly fell into the closest bell. "What?"

"Does that look like a *P*?" He squinted. It certainly did. "Get your knife out and see if you can wiggle the stone free."

He attacked the mortar, chipping it loose with savage thrusts. Bits of rock skittered across the floor, some falling through the open window slats, though no one would notice unless they landed on their head. As the stone's edges were exposed, he jammed his blade in and searched for purchase, never quite getting enough grip to move it. Pain lanced into his shoulders and dryness crept across his tongue. At last, one blow struck solidly and dislodged a thick chunk of mortar.

"Careful." Jane grabbed a chunk of debris after it clanged off a bell. "Don't drop this out of the window or let it hit the bell. If anyone hears us, we'll be trapped here."

"Stand back. Catch this if it falls." With his blade locked in the wall, he wiggled it back and forth; the stone moved ever so slightly. Grit and dirt crumbled as he pulled. Then, without warning, the rock gave way, crashing to the floor before Jane could corral it. Parker squinted into the new hole. *Jane was right.* James had been here, had carved his initial into the stone, and left something behind – a small leather pouch.

"It feels oily." Parker grabbed the dark sack and pulled it out, the leather soft in his palm. "Can we open it?"

Jane snatched it from him. "Hold the light."

Before Parker could protest, she jammed her phone into his hand and opened the bag. "More leather paper, folded." A much lighter piece of cowhide came out. Jane held it up to the dim sunlight, then leaned toward Parker. "Give me more light." Familiar handwriting came to life, the same neat, spidery letters he'd seen before.

Philip,

I have lost those who seek these honours. I know of a safe place for storage, where you will find them waiting should I not return. Visit the house on shepherd's hill, where the hound and horn announce death's arrival. Below ground, by the water, you will find everything.

James

"Does *house on shepherd's hill* mean anything to you?" Parker asked.

"No more than *hound and horn announce death's arrival* does. Whatever it means, there must be water nearby." Jane coughed, shaking her head. "We can research it later. No need to stay here any longer."

"You won't be going anywhere." A new voice boomed through the bell tower, seeming to come from every direction. "If you move, I shoot."

The ladder. A gun pointed at them from atop the narrow wooden rise, at the end of which a ghost waited.

"Christopher Jankowski." Parker said it without thinking.

The man clambered uneasily to the top floor, limping as he moved. Bruising surrounded one eye, and a bandage was wrapped around his empty hand. "How do you know my name?" he asked, scowling.

Shit. Bad move. Parker edged toward Jane. "You dropped an inhaler at Stirling Castle. The police got your name from it." Not quite true, but if he thought the cops knew who he was, it made killing them riskier. "They know you tried to kill us."

Jankowski's face twisted. "If you went to the police, why aren't they here?"

Jane jumped in. "They're not interested in scraps of writing or old theories. Catching two gunmen is what they care about." That gave him another pause. Jankowski stepped forward, squinting as the sunlight hit his eyes. Parker touched Jane's elbow and pulled her back a step, putting the bells between them and the gun.

"Stop moving!" Jankowski waved the gun and came at them. "Stay there or I shoot!" Slashes of dark and light flashed across his face, bright moving tattoos. When sunlight painted his entire jaw, Parker shoved Jane. Jankowski stepped forward, directly into a blinding patch of light.

The gunshot boomed off stone walls as the bullet went wide, a bell sparking as Parker tackled Jane to the ground. "Go around!" he shouted in her ear. At least he thought he shouted. Everything sounded like he had cotton in his ears. Jane scrambled away, scooting on all fours. Parker backed against the bell, the metal still vibrating from Jankowski's bullet.

If I can't hear, then he can't either. Parker leaned around the bell and looked directly down a pistol barrel. The gun boomed again and a bullet whizzed past his face, shattering stone on the wall across from him. Shards dinged off the metal at his back as Parker dove for cover, searing pain slashing through his hand as he left a trail of red palm prints on the floorboards. He'd ripped his palm on the stone he'd levered out of the wall. Sharp but round, it resembled nothing so much as a rock baseball. Wiping the blood from his wound, he squinted at the rock and then at Jankowski. No more than ten feet separated Parker and the shooter. *I can hit him.* Stand up, pull back and fire the rock at Jankowski's head.

Parker spotted Jane between two bells and held up a hand. *Stay put.* He darted around the far side toward Jankowski. Unless he wanted to wager their lives on a thrown rock, he needed to get up close and smash the guy's head. Even after months in dingy bars, the muscles in his arm felt capable. He edged around the second bell and spotted Jankowski moving toward Jane, gun leading the way.

As Jankowski's finger tightened on the trigger, Parker jumped up and shouted. "Hey!"

It bought him the split second he needed. Jankowski looked over and Parker whipped the rock at the gunman's head. It whizzed by as the gun swung toward Parker and Jane grabbed hold of Jankowski's bicep. He punched at her with his free hand to send Jane staggering against the wall. But Parker was airborne, headed for Jankowski's chest at full speed. He smashed into the gunman and they crashed to the floor in a heap. Dust burned his eyes and the wind was knocked out of him as he lost his grip on Jankowski. Parker rolled away and smacked into a bell, panic seizing him as he waited for the next shot.

Instead of gunfire, a cry filled the air, loud at first then fading. Through the dust Parker saw blue skies, wide and clear. *Where'd the window go?* Only when Jane ran toward him did he realize Jankowski had fallen through one of the tower windows.

Jane leaned outside. "He's dead."

Parker grabbed for purchase on the bell, found none, and slid back down. "Good." Only when he got his feet beneath him did the world swim back into focus. "Bastard wanted us dead."

"People are gathering down there."

"You have the message?" She nodded, and he headed for the door. "Let's get out of here before the cops show up." He had one foot already out the door when an idea struck him. "Wait – I need to see the body." He headed off without explaining, taking the steps down two at a time as Jane ran behind him. Around and around they went, spinning until sunlight warmed his face and the growing crowd of bystanders blocked the way. Sirens wailed in the distance, getting louder.

"Move aside." Parker bulled his way to the center. "I know CPR." He made it through, though one glance showed Jankowski needed more than chest compressions. One leg stuck out at an unnatural angle. A trickle of blood dripped from his nose, and his forehead looked strangely compressed. He wasn't breathing.

"Move back." Parker glared, and space formed around the body. The sirens screamed as he leaned over Jankowski's chest, doing his best to hide that he was rummaging through the gunman's pockets. His second try struck gold.

"Give him room!" someone yelled. "Where's the ambulance?"

Any replies were lost as Parker ducked back into the crowd. Head low, he grabbed Jane's arm without slowing. "Move." They walked onto the sidewalk and behind a group of trees as the medics arrived.

By the time a second ambulance raced past, Parker and Jane were a block away.

"You are crazy," Jane said when they made it to her car. Arms crossed on her chest, she made no move to unlock it. "Why did you do that?"

"Look what I got." He displayed Jankowski's cell phone and wallet. "Now we can find out who's after us, and how they knew we'd be here."

Jane threw her arms up. "Who cares? We have to stop this before we're killed. We can't find what James left behind if we're dead." Her arms went back down. "We have no idea if there is even anything at the end of all this, whatever *this* is."

"You want to give up?"

She tried to fight it for a minute, but no, not after what they'd been through, and not after what Parker had seen in her. The same spirit and drive as Erika. Jane glared at him. "I didn't say that."

"Good. Now get in the car."

Moments later they sped away from the campus, headed to anyplace where cops wouldn't be looking for a man and woman fitting their description. It was unlikely any bystanders had gotten a good enough look at Parker to identify him, but you never knew. Several people had pulled out their cell phones and filmed the scene, more interested in recording a stranger's demise than helping him.

"What if the phone has a password?" Jane asked.

"I already checked. It does."

"Then how are you going to open it?"

"I used his thumbprint to unlock it." Parker swerved into a parking lot and held up the iPhone. "Same way I unlock mine."

Jane's mouth opened, then closed. He gave her a second. "How did you know to do that?" She finally asked.

"Educated guess. You know, the things you historians make all the time." She actually smiled at that. "I also grabbed his wallet. Figured it may help us find who's paying his bills." He rifled through the wallet first. "Or not. Cash, but not much else." About a thousand euro, which Parker set in a cup holder. "He won't need it."

"What about the phone?" Jane asked.

"Three text messages, all from blocked numbers. Listen to the first one," Parker said, and read it aloud. "*Go to Stirling Castle.*" He looked up. "That's the wrong place. Who would have told him?"

Jane shook her head. "Not Evan. He couldn't be involved, no matter what you think. How would he even know people like this?"

"You may be right. Listen to the next one. *They are headed to St. Andrews. New vehicle is a Mercedes.'* It gives the color, but no tags, so it may be that Evan didn't sell us out. If he wanted to tell these guys where to find us, he's smart enough to check your plates before we left."

"If he knew where I parked," Jane said. "When was the first message sent?"

"About thirty minutes after we got on the road." Not good for Evan, but Jane wasn't swayed.

"It could be a coincidence." Parker opened his mouth to object. "But," she said, cutting him off, "it could also be something else. How do you explain the second message sending him to St. Andrews?"

Parker shrugged. "I can't. All this tells us is that about thirty minutes after the first message, Jankowski learns our real destination. How is beyond me." He scrolled to the final text message and frowned. "This is strange. He got a text less than twenty minutes ago telling him to check his email immediately."

"Even though he's chasing us? Must be an important email."

"I'll tell you in a second." Parker scrolled to Jankowski's inbox. "This guy was thorough about deleting emails. There's only one." Parker tapped on it and his eyes narrowed. "It's a set of instructions, but it doesn't seem to be about us. Something about a stone and Glasgow." His own phone buzzed before he could read any farther. "Nick's calling," he said, and connected it.

"Glad to hear you're still alive," Nick said. "Anything happen to you lately?"

"Is that a joke?"

"You lead an interesting life. Too interesting to be very long, if you want my opinion." His tone grew serious. "Did you run into more trouble?" Parker recounted their attack in the bell tower and the dead assailant. "Good move on checking the body," Nick said.

"We now have proof someone is selling us out."

Parker relayed the messages and Nick agreed. "Someone is able to give away your location. If you think one of Jane's coworkers is involved, they must also have a way of tracking her after she leaves the campus. How else would they know Stirling wasn't the right place?" Nick fell silent, and Parker waited. "Are you in a university car now?" Nick asked.

"No, we have one of her family cars. But anyone on campus could have seen her pull up in it."

"What about your electronics – a cell phone or laptop?"

Parker turned to Jane. "Is your phone a work or private one?"

"I have both." She displayed two identical phones. "One from the university and one I pay for myself."

"You hear that?" Parker asked Nick.

"Tracking cell phones is easy," Nick said, "if you have the right equipment."

Parker grabbed Jane's work phone and pulled it apart. "I just took her battery out," he said.

"Toss it out the window, preferably into another vehicle heading the opposite direction."

Parker's window buzzed down and her cell phone flew out, lost in the roadside grasses. Jane reached for it far too late. "What was that for?"

"So no one can track us," he said. "I'll buy you a new one." She grumbled, but her heart wasn't in it.

"That will slow down anyone using it to follow you," Nick said.

"No need to toss her personal phone, but keep it powered off." By now he was on speakerphone, so Jane did as he ordered. "Find anything else on the dead man's phone?"

"One email," Parker said. "There's no junk mail or credit card bills. Nothing but this. I'll read it." He opened the email again. "It's weird."

"I'm all ears."

Parker started reading. "*Our client is interested in rumors she heard about the stone. Suspicion exists the real one is still lost, replaced after the theft and damage. Go to Glasgow and convince the mason to reveal the truth.*" He read through the message again, and it still made no sense. "You have any idea what he's talking about?"

Nick didn't, but Jane did. "I do." She took a deep breath. "Have you ever heard of the Stone of Scone?" Parker and Nick both said they hadn't. "It's an important artifact in both Scottish and English history. The stone has been used for enthroning monarchs for over eight hundred years," she said. "Originally Scottish monarchs sat on it for their coronation, but that ended when Edward I captured the stone and took it to London."

"What's so important about it?" Nick asked.

"If you believe the legends, it dates to biblical times in Scotland. While the stone itself is unremarkable, the history associated with it is anything but."

"Is it valuable?" Nick asked.

"Somewhere between worthless and priceless. Easily millions to the right collector, probably someone who would keep it in a vault. The last time it was used officially was at Queen Elizabeth's coronation in 1953."

"Where is it now?" Parker asked.

"In Edinburgh, on public display."

"Any reason to think it's not real? What would they mean by *theft* and *damage*?"

"The stone was kept at Westminster Abbey until 1950, when four

Scottish students stole it and brought it back to Scotland as part of a political protest. Being such capable criminals, these kids dropped the stone and it broke in half. They buried part of it in a field and hid the other half in their car. Eventually they took both pieces to a stonemason in Glasgow for repairs, and then they left it at a church and called the police, who took the stone back to Westminster. It was there until England returned it to Scotland in 1996. Since then it's been on display at Edinburgh Castle with the Crown Jewels."

"Were there rumors it was a fake?" Nick asked.

"Not really," Jane said after a moment's thought. "You hear baseless theories about many artifacts, but nothing reliable. The stone is large, heavy and hard to move. College students stole it, not professional thieves, and they were about as inept as could be."

"Still, someone thinks this could be true, and that someone has the resources to send armed men after you two," Nick said. "Maybe it's nonsense, or maybe they're on to something. Either way, what matters is keeping your heads down and away from bullets."

"We have to pin down who's selling us out," Parker said. "It's someone we know."

"Maybe," Nick said. "Or the person or people doing this could be on a beach in the Caribbean right now. Proximity isn't required to track your movements. Either way, you should get to a safe place and lay low."

"We're headed back to Jane's castle now. As far as places go, it's fairly defensible." She narrowed her eyes at him. Parker bit back a smile. "We need to decipher this latest message."

"Before you do that, I have one other thing. Do you remember the artifacts smuggling I mentioned to you?"

"That group spread across Scotland and England," Parker said. "You said you know people investigating it."

"I dug into the case files, and we suspect there's one main player in Scotland who is funding the break-ins and thefts. The evidence indicates they're not averse to killing to get what they want."

Parker raised an eyebrow. "That's not much to go on."

"This person is very good," Nick said. "Money trails dry up, informants either won't talk or don't know anything, and anything illegal is kept at arm's length from them. They don't get their hands dirty."

"You're saying we could be in over our heads?" Jane asked.

"Pretty much. I doubt you'll listen, but don't do anything stupid. Whatever you're chasing isn't worth dying over."

"We'll let you know what we find," Parker said. Nick promised to do the same before clicking off. He turned to Jane, who held the wheel tightly. "Scared yet?"

"Of course I am. I'd be daft if I wasn't, but that doesn't mean it's time to give up." Gooseflesh rose on her forearms. "Even though I know this is crazy, it's unlike anything I've experienced in academia." Her voice dropped. "I've worked with dusty documents and scraps of pottery for years, things most people consider junk, but for me, it's the best story of all. The past speaks to us in different ways, some of them hard to hear. If you listen, though, it's an amazing tale. For it to happen in real time, for me to be a part of it, I can't tell you what it's like." Her face lit up as she turned to him. "You must think I've lost my mind."

No, he didn't. Jane wasn't the first person to look at him this way. "I don't know exactly how you feel, but I know what you mean. There's no chance in hell you're giving up."

"I couldn't even if I wanted to."

Parker raised a hand, and she slapped him five. "Then let's figure out what James is talking about." He reached for the pouch.

"There's one other thing you should know," Jane said. "About the Stone of Scone. What made me connect the email and the stone was the Glasgow stonemason reference."

"Why is that?"

"You don't know this, but Hugh is from Glasgow."

Parker shrugged. "Glasgow's a big city."

"Yes, but not all of its inhabitants live to be as old as Hugh. He's close to ninety."

Parker remembered the man's iron grip and muscular forearms, impressive even now. "I can't imagine what he was like back in the day."

"Hugh was strong then and he still is. However, what I'm getting at is Hugh knows people in Glasgow. Including one stonemason."

"He knows the man who fixed the stone?"

Jane nodded. "They lived near each other. Both their fathers worked in the shipyards."

"How do you know this?"

"Hugh told me," she said. "When I first learned about the Stone of Scone, he mentioned how an old friend of his was involved with the story. A century ago Glasgow had only a few major industries. One was shipbuilding, so the fact Hugh's family knew this stonemason and his family isn't that unusual. What's more interesting is they've both survived this long. A life of manual labor may keep you strong, but it's hell on your body. People wear out after decades of hard work like that. Not to mention the drinking those men did."

"Do you think Hugh would talk to this man for us? He could at least warn him about what we found."

"I'm sure Hugh won't mind calling an old friend if I ask."

"We should let Hugh read the message for himself."

Jane grinned. "He'll be thrilled." They sped up, and the road slipped by in a blur. Barnbougle Castle soon appeared in the distance, holding the falling sun above its rocky roof. Jane had called ahead, and they pulled around back to find Hugh waiting on the porch holding a double-barreled shotgun.

Jane jumped out of the car. "Is everything okay?"

"Right as rain." He tapped the stock. "An old man can't clean his hunting guns?"

Parker didn't believe him for a second, but the sight of Hugh carrying the lethal piece was comforting. Anybody looking to cause trouble here would have a fight on their hands. For now, however, nothing but a warm breeze and the soft lap of water on the shoreline followed them inside before Hugh secured the door and closed the deadbolt.

"I hope you had a nice trip to St. Andrew's." They stood around a table, Hugh leaving the shotgun within arm's reach. "Didn't miss a thing here. Quiet as can be, other than the utilities men coming by. One of the neighbors' line poles cracked, so they checked all of them in the area. They don't want one falling on anyone's house."

"Good thing," Jane said, and then cut to the chase. "We were right. James did go to St. Salvator's bell tower, and he left another message."

"Did you run into any trouble?" Hugh may as well have been asking about a dentist appointment.

"You could say that." She detailed Parker's battle with Jankowski, his tumble out the window, and the subsequent body search. "His phone had several surprises, which we can discuss in a minute. I'd rather you read the message first." She pushed the leather pouch toward him.

With a delicate touch belying his calloused palms, Hugh opened the drawstring. "What have we here?" The piece of leather paper emerged. Reciting the message, Hugh held the paper between thumb and forefinger as though it could disintegrate at any moment. "I must say, Jane, this means nothing to me."

"Read it again. Out loud."

Hugh took a deep breath. "*I have lost those who seek these honours. I know of a safe place for storage, where you will find them waiting should I not return. Visit the house on shepherd's hill, where the hound and horn announce death's arrival. Below ground, by S.W. and the water, you will find everything.*"

Hugh looked up. "He keeps talking about *honours*, whatever that means. Doesn't strike a chord."

"An honor isn't tangible," Parker said. "You can't physically hold it, and it sounds like James is carrying these with him. It could be a title of some kind, maybe a noble appointment with land or money attached."

"A piece of paper that makes the bearer a titled landowner?" Hugh asked.

"I never thought of that," Jane said. "It could be, depending on the title." Her hand settled on the forest of white hair covering his forearm. "Good idea."

"Is there a specific area in Scotland famous for its sheep or shepherding?" Parker asked.

Hugh chuckled. "Tough to answer, young man. Hard to find a place *not* involved with them." He rustled his great white beard. "If I had to pick, my guess would be the Highlands. Wild sheep everywhere."

Jane tapped the table. "What about Inverness? It's basically the Highland capital, and it's certainly on a hill."

Hugh nodded. "Could be. If you think about that city, one place comes to mind."

"Inverness Castle," Jane said. "It makes sense."

Parker raised a hand. "Let's assume we're not all Scottish. What are the Highlands, and where is Inverness Castle?"

"The Highlands cover nearly half of Scotland," Jane said.

"That narrows it down."

"The area is mountainous," she said, ignoring him. "Which accounts for the *hill* reference. Not many people live there, but most are in Inverness."

"Could James have visited the city?"

She nodded. "Inverness is closer to central Scotland than most other Highlands locations. We can drive there in a few hours, but it would have taken James several days."

"A trip he could have made."

Jane nodded. "It also has plenty of wild sheep, and the city is over a thousand years old."

"Sounds like a good place to hide if people were chasing you."

"And to hide something you didn't want others to find." She turned to Hugh. "I'll check it out."

Parker wasn't sure, but it was possible a smile had formed beneath Hugh's beard. "Any idea about the hound and horn?"

"That phrase practically screams *legend*," Jane said. "If I find anything about a hound or a horn and impending death, we are in business." She pointed to the final line. "The last part is the best. *You will find everything.* Sounds to me like James finally got rid of these *honours* he keeps mentioning. Too bad there are more lochs and rivers in this country than we can count. And about the *S.W.*, I have no idea."

"One problem at a time, my dear." Hugh pointed to her head. "You use that glorious education of yours and see what can be found first. Then the light may shine on what's next."

Jane patted his hand. "Always the positive one. I have a favor to ask."

"A favor from old Hugh? Whatever could it be?"

Birds chirped outside, their chatter seeming to warm the cool castle air. "Do you remember telling me about the Stone of Scone?"

"Do I remember?" A chair rattled across the flagstones and Hugh sat down, looking into the crackling fire. "You loved that tale. Must have asked me to tell it a hundred times if it was once." Hugh turned back from the hearth. "Now why mention such an old memory? I can't imagine you forgot what happened."

"It's part of what we found today."

"When I grabbed his cell phone and checked his email," Parker said, "there was only one message in it."

Jane picked up for him. "A message I think relates to the Stone of Scone."

The words sent Hugh back in his chair. "This dead man was interested in the Stone?"

"His employer was." She brought him up to date on Parker's friendship with Nick Dean and the suspected artifact smuggling ring in Scotland, which Nick had tied back to one person. "We think Jankowski was supposed to do something involving the Stone after he dealt with Parker and me."

"All he had to do is go to Edinburgh Castle," Hugh said. "You know that. It's on display for everyone to see alongside the Crown Jewels."

"Whoever sent this message doesn't think so," Jane said. "Show him." Parker turned the phone's screen toward Hugh. "Someone believes the stone on display is a fake. They told Jankowski to find the real one."

"They were going to see Bertie." Hugh's words were scarcely audible. "That's why you asked. They were going to Glasgow to see my old mate."

"You and Robert are friends," Jane said. "Do you still speak with him?"

"Not for years. Bertie isn't much of a talker. Could be he isn't even alive."

"Do you have any way to contact him?" Parker asked.

"I might," Hugh said. "Jane, would you get my notebook from my desk?" Jane darted down the hallway, leaving Parker alone with Hugh. The old man stared at the table, and he still hadn't moved when Jane returned with the book. "I'll need the phone." Slipping on a pair of reading glasses, he flipped the well-worn pages until one caught his eye. "Here it is. Bertie's number."

"Would you call him for us?" Jane asked. "Even if he doesn't want to talk, at least you can warn him."

Hugh chuckled as he dialed. "The first person who shows up at Bertie's door with a gun will have a hard time of it. He's mean as a cornered jackal. More than once we got in a scrape at the pub, and I don't think anyone ever topped him." Hugh held the phone to his ear. Several beats passed before he spoke. "I'm looking for Bertie Gray. Tell him Hugh is calling. Hugh from the neighborhood." Hugh covered the mouthpiece. "Sounds like the old bugger is still kicking."

"I'd like to speak with him if he's up for it," Jane said.

Hugh made a circle with his thumb and forefinger. "I will take care of it." After a solid minute passed in silence, noise came from the phone. "Yes, this is Hugh. Bertie, is that you?" Hugh winked at Jane. "Bertie, you old dog. Yes, Hugh from Glasgow. No, not dead yet. Sounds like you aren't either. Listen, I have to tell you something. It's important. Actually, a friend of mine wants to speak with you." Hugh's head shook. "No, not a reporter. I work for her. We think you may be in danger." A noise like a car backfiring came from the phone. "This is not a joke, Bertie. It's about the rock you fixed." Silence ensued. "Bertie, are you there?" More growls. "Hold on, I need a pen." He motioned to Jane with his hand.

Jane handed over a pen and paper. "Go ahead," Hugh said, and started scribbling. "Right. I'll tell them. You'll be there tomorrow? Good. Take care of yourself, mate." Hugh hung up and pushed the notepaper to Jane. "Bertie doesn't like to talk about the past. Said the only way he'll do it is if you come to him. Too many story hounds and curiosity seekers have passed his way over the years, and he's had enough."

"Then why will he speak with us?" Jane asked.

"Old ties run strong in Glasgow. Bertie will have a chat for my sake," and here he leaned closer, "but my advice is get moving before he changes his mind."

Jane turned to Parker. "Are you free tomorrow?"

"I'll be here first thing in the morning." Parker raised his arms over his head, casting a long shadow as the sunlight warmed his face through a tall window. Right now, the thought of his bed was a powerful draw. "I'll head home and be back here at sunrise. I'm sure Bertie gets up pretty early."

"It's just over an hour from here to Glasgow." Jane slipped Bertie's address into her pocket. "I'm not tired yet, so I'll look into the Highlands angle, try to figure out if James is really pointing to Inverness as the next stop." Any trace of fatigue disappeared as she spoke. "We can afford a day to look into this Stone of Scone question, but I don't want James's trail going cold."

"It's been waiting for three centuries," Parker said. "Another day won't hurt." He stopped halfway to the door. "Keep the doors locked."

"Nobody will be around without me knowing," Hugh said. One hand went for the shotgun. "It's time I cleaned all the hunting equipment, I believe. Even old man White's family gun should be dusted." He nodded to the massive weapon hanging over the crackling fire. "Wouldn't want it to rust."

"No, you wouldn't." Parker's keys jangled in his hand. "I'll bring coffee tomorrow." With that, he stepped out and pulled the front door shut. Hugh could handle security. With nearly a century of experience, he could fend off anyone coming for trouble at this castle. Parker couldn't help but grin. He'd been in his share of scraps, and he had no desire to mess with Hugh. Men like him didn't die easily.

Chapter 11

Barnbougle Castle
July 10th

Gravel crunched under the Mustang's tires as Parker pulled up in front of Jane's castle, nearly spilling three cups of coffee at the same time as he tried to balance them all with one hand. He'd nearly overslept, forcing him to fall back on the rubber band again to tie back his wet hair. He really needed a cut. Cursing as he walked, Parker reached for the front door only to have it open before him. Jane grabbed two of the cups and twisted him back around at the same time.

"The car is packed," she said. "It's around back. Hugh and I will be out in a second." With that, the door slammed in his face. Holy cow, but Jane had energy, and it was contagious.

Hugh stepped out from a side door. Instead of a shotgun, he clutched a steaming cup, which he raised toward Parker in a salute. "Welcome, and thank you for the coffee. I hope you had a restful evening."

"I did. Are the guns all clean?"

"Ready for action," Hugh said. "The evening proved uneventful."

"Good to hear."

Jane bounded out between them, tossing a backpack into Parker's arms. "Toss that in the boot, would you?" She turned back to Hugh as Parker fumbled with the pack. "We should be back by this evening."

"I'll manage." Hugh tenderly patted her back. "Give Bertie my regards, and tell him I will be by to visit before long."

"Sure you don't want to come?"

"Certain. This old horse will enjoy a midday nap as usual, so don't ring the doorbell when you return."

They drove off with Jane at the wheel of yet another vehicle – this time a Land Rover – and Hugh fading into the distance, a sentinel watching over the castle. The engine purred as they took a direct route to Glasgow. Parker lowered the sun visor as Jane found the motorway and merged into the passing lane.

"I slept like a rock last night," he said. "Any luck with the Inverness angle?"

"Yes and no," she said. "Sheep have been associated with the Highlands for centuries. They roam wild in the countryside, and if we put ourselves in James's shoes, Inverness is the town where he's most likely to place anything he wanted to hide well."

"Do you think he hid these *honours* near water by Inverness Castle?"

"Without actually visiting the area, I can't tell what the most likely spots are. My first thought runs toward a permanent structure, a building or location associated with sheep in some way. Perhaps a marketplace?" She shrugged. "I just don't know. I'll have a better idea once we look around."

"If it's another piece of paper, James could have hidden it almost anywhere." In his mind, he ran through the hiding spots they'd uncovered so far. "In a building by the river or castle is a good idea. Maybe a nearby church? It would have to be somewhere both James and Philip could access, a place that wouldn't change overnight."

"Or it could be inside the castle itself," Jane said. "We can't assume James didn't have access to it, even though it's unlikely."

"Is the castle open to tourists now?"

"Only the grounds. The actual castle houses part of the court system."

"So at least it will be a short trip if we get arrested," Parker said. "Let's start at the castle and see where it leads. You never know; the answer could jump out and bite us while we're walking around."

Jane's eyes narrowed. "Counting on luck is a fool's errand."

"Never hurts to be optimistic, but I agree." A more pressing concern weighed on his mind. "Any idea how to get an old man to talk about something he seems eager to forget?"

The scowl on her face flipped right-side up. "Leave that to me. I've been around Hugh long enough to know how to get this guy to talk."

"How's that?"

"Check the bag behind your seat."

Parker reached around and found a paper bag. Inside it was a glass bottle. "Single malt whiskey? Very nice."

"Recognize the distillery?"

He studied the label more closely. "Bowmore." Then he saw the age. "This isn't just a single malt."

"Bowmore Single Malt, aged twenty-five years. Be careful with it." She negotiated a curve, and his hands tightened on the bag. "Nothing like world-class whiskey to start conversation. You should hear Hugh's stories after a glass of this stuff. The hardest part is getting him to stop before the sun comes up."

"I like your plan."

"Thank you." Jane cleared her throat, and Parker caught her glancing over at him. "I used the university database last night. I had to log on to the internal school network."

"Which means people could see what you researched."

"Someone with administrative access could see I researched Inverness," she said. "I also searched for information on Glasgow, William Wallace, Stirling Bridge, and Northern Ireland. Good luck to anybody trying to decipher my true intentions." Jane zipped around a bus. "There's more," she said. "I've received dozens of emails in the past few days, but two caught my eye. One was from Evan Ford."

"What did he want?"

"He asked what my schedule is for the week." Her voice dropped. "Specifically, where I would be today and tomorrow. Don't worry," she said when he frowned. "I didn't respond. It's really none of his business."

"Hopefully your search history keeps him going in circles."

"*If* he's the one involved with this. There's no proof Evan is tracking me."

"No proof he isn't, either," Parker grumbled. "What was the other email?"

"Tom Gregan asked if my phone is in order. He couldn't reach me regarding our monthly staff meeting and became concerned. I told him I forgot to charge it."

"Is that unusual?"

"Not at all, considering I'm supposed to attend the meeting. It slipped my mind."

"Did you tell him where you're going today?"

"No. I took a vacation day to focus on my work without any office distractions. Tom won't expect to see or hear from me until tomorrow."

"I'd still keep your phone off," Parker said. "Just to be safe."

Jane snapped her fingers. "I almost forgot. I asked Evan to research several topics for me, including the bit about the shepherd's hill, and the horn and hound part. He may as well do it while I'm gone. There's no way he can connect the research with James's path, considering I gave him three other topics to study."

The idea sent an uneasy ripple through Parker's stomach. Too late to undo it now. "What else did Hugh tell you about his friend?"

"Not much more than what you heard. Bertie dabbled in politics after the Stone of Scone business. Hugh said he's 'as crotchety a bastard as ever lived, and the best mate you could ask for.' Sounds like a solid fellow."

"Let's hope he's in a sharing mood."

"Have faith, Parker. We'll get Mr. Gray to share his story."

Green grasses of varying intensity covered the ground on either side of them as they motored toward Glasgow, from the hilltops soaked in sunlight to the valleys dark with shade stealing the light to make Scotland's countryside uniquely beautiful. Farmsteads and gravel roads turned to suburbia and named side streets, soon giving way to traffic and homes so close they breathed on each other. The city swallowed them whole; their vehicle quickly lost in a maze of narrow streets and similar neighborhoods. Jane turned into a wide lane that pointed straight to the river's edge, where two buildings waited at the end. Bertie's place.

A gravel parking lot fronted the larger structure, two stories high with glass windows reflecting liquid fire. Across a narrow driveway Parker spotted a large boat at the dock. What could only be Robert Gray's home stood alone, looking much happier for the space it had on either side.

"Big yard he has here," said Parker.

"It's his home and his business. Let's start with the business side," Jane said. "That's where he was when Hugh called."

A bell jangled as Parker opened the shop's front door, the loudest noise in a massive garage of silent machines meant for scraping, cutting and shaping rock, all contained under a single roof. Close to where they stood, a sleeping dog snuffled at the sound of their footsteps, barely opening his eyes before he started snoring again, his tail perilously close to the rocking chair behind him. Unlike his canine friend, the man sitting quite still in the chair gazed directly at them.

A voice leathered by countless cigarettes offered a greeting. "Sales room is next door."

Jane was undeterred. "We are looking for Robert Gray. I'm a friend of Hugh Burton's."

The rocking chair ceased moving. "That so?"

Jane nodded. "Yes. We came from Edinburgh to speak with him."

"Robert Gray is a tired, old man. Come back after lunch."

After lunch? They had driven the whole way out here, and this guy wouldn't tell them where to find Gray for another five hours? The hell with this. Parker opened his mouth, but Jane stopped him.

"I'm told Robert Gray is 'as crotchety a bastard as ever lived'." She walked over to the man. The dog noted her approach and, in his best guard dog impression, rolled over for a tummy rub. His tail thumped the floor when Jane obliged. "I'm also told Robert Gray is 'the best mate you could ask for.' That sounds like a man I want to share a drink with."

What could have been a smile flickered across the old man's lined features. The pace of his rocking picked up. "You tell that no-good Hugh Burton he's worse, and he cannot handle his drink at that." His eyes flicked open as the paper bag crinkled and the bottle of expensive whiskey appeared. "Did Hugh send that?"

"No," Jane said. "I figured you for a single-malt man on my own."

This time Bertie Gray did smile, his eyes alight beneath two unruly hedges of white. "You figured right, young lady." He pointed his cane at two chairs beside him, then at a small table nearby. "Sit."

Parker slid the chairs around the table in front of Bertie.

"See the bell?" Bertie asked, and Parker nodded. "Ring it for me." Parker obliged, and a man walked through the shop door, dusting his hands off.

"Yes, Mr. Gray?"

"Tea for my visitors," Bertie said. "And cheese." The man nodded and disappeared back out the door. "Stop wasting time." Bertie reached over and tapped the table with his cane. "The whiskey has aged long enough. Use those muscles of yours, young fellow, and pour an old man a drink." Parker opened the bottle and then stopped and peered around the room. "Glasses are underneath." Sure enough, three glasses were tucked on a shelf below, and Parker filled them all.

"Just a dash for me," Jane said. "I'm driving."

Bertie harrumphed. "More for us, then." He brought his glass to his lips, peering at Parker and Jane over the rim. "Certain people say gentlemen don't drink before lunch. I say you don't want people like that in your life." He tipped his drink toward them both. "*Sláinte.*" With that, a good portion of the expensive whiskey vanished.

"*Sláinte,*" Parker said, and sipped. As peaty smoke warmed his belly. Footsteps clicked on the shop floor and he looked up to find a woman carrying food on a platter.

"Cheese, Mr. Gray." She settled the tray on the table; at least four kinds of cheese were spread across it, accompanied by an assortment of biscuits. "Tea will be along."

"Forgive me," Jane said after the woman left. "I never properly introduced myself." She stuck her hand out, and Bertie studied it. "Jane White."

He managed to shake her hand without setting down either his whiskey or his cane. "What's Hugh doing now?"

"Hugh is the caretaker of our home. I've known him my entire life."

"More than a house if you need a caretaker," Bertie fired back.

Parker laughed behind his glass, ignoring Jane's stare. "It's home to us," she said. "But yes, it is spacious. My family owns Barnbougle Castle."

"And a fine home it must be," Bertie said. He inclined his head toward Parker. "What is your name, young fellow with the long hair?"

Parker couldn't tell if Bertie was looking straight at him or not, not with those bushy eyebrows in the way. "Parker. Parker Chase." His hand went out, and a grip like steel crushed it. What was it with these old Scottish guys and their handshakes? "Jane and my fiancée were classmates."

Now Bertie definitely looked his way. He sipped again, watching Parker all the while. "What brings you from Edinburgh on such a morning as this? If it's a story you seek, I'm done with that. It's been told enough."

"Not this part of it." Jane took her first sip of whiskey and leaned over the table. "First, we have a story for you. Then you decide if you want to talk." Before she could begin, the woman reappeared with a tea service, depositing it on the table and leaving without a word.

"Would you like me to pour the tea?" Parker asked.

Again the stare, which stretched on and on. Bertie's cane finally tapped the floor. "Two sugars, lemon. Pour yourself first." Feeling as though he'd passed some kind of test, Parker poured a cup for each of them. When he sipped the scalding hot beverage, he found he couldn't taste anything but the remnants of good whiskey. "It's delicious."

"The only thing the English do better than us." Bertie didn't touch his tea, holding the whiskey tight. "Go ahead, Jane. Tell me your story."

"First, can you keep a secret?"

Bertie winked. "Better than most."

"Good." Jane launched into the tale, starting with the letter Parker had found in a skeleton's shirt and ending with the assailant who'd fallen from a bell tower at St. Andrews. "Parker grabbed a cell phone from the man's pocket, and that's where we found the message."

The old man didn't react much, other than taking a bite of cheese. He chewed slowly, his eyes on Parker. "How did you get the phone?" Bertie asked.

"I grabbed it just before the paramedics arrived," Parker said. "Nobody noticed."

Another harrumph, possibly of approval this time. "An interesting story." He jiggled his empty glass, nodding at the bottle. "Why do you think this message involves me?" he asked as Parker refilled it.

Jane sipped her tea. "I'm almost certain the message references the Stone of Scone. The dead man's name was Jankowski, and we know he worked for someone who traffics in stolen artifacts." She recited the email from memory.

"*Our client is interested in rumors she heard about the stone. Suspicion exists the real one is still lost, replaced after the theft and damage. Go to Glasgow and convince the mason to reveal the truth."*

No harrumph this time. "And you think I'm the Glasgow mason?"

"It makes sense." Jane twisted the napkin in her hands. "What other stone artifact has been stolen, damaged, and then repaired?"

"Dozens come through here," Bertie said. "Gravestones, for one, and quite a few other kinds."

"Point taken, except none of them would interest a high-end black-market collector. Whoever hired Jankowski was willing to kill to get their hands on these *honours*, and we're not even sure what they are."

"I learned long ago people are capable of horrible things for little reason." Bertie pointed to the tea tray. "Pass me a biscuit? You may be right. Or could be wrong. All I know is I wish that damn stone had never darkened my door for the trouble it's caused." He cast an arm around the room. "Trying to run a business, and people show up every week wanting to talk about it. Slowed down as of late, but they never stop. All I did was patch the damn thing, and now it follows me for decades."

Parker took care to fill the empty whiskey glasses before speaking. "Did you ever hear a rumor that the stone in Edinburgh is fake?"

"People don't want the truth. They want a conspiracy, a new chapter in the story, when it's been dead and buried since before you were born." A tinge of emotion colored his words. Bertie sat up straighter as one age-spotted hand curled into a fist. "Every time, I tell them the same thing." Parker and Jane remained silent as the summer breeze carried floral notes through the open windows.

"The stone I repaired is gone." Bertie's cane thudded. "Given back to those who stole it, and then returned. Fixed good as new."

"The men who stole it brought it in two pieces, didn't they?" Bertie nodded to Jane. "Did you know what it was when they came here?" she asked.

"Every lad knows about the Stone," Bertie said. "And those *boys*, for they were not more than that, did not pay for my questions. They came to the best stonemason in Glasgow, and that is what they got."

"What did it look like?" Parker asked.

"You have not seen it?" Parker said he hadn't. "Then get up, young man, get up. You have come to the right place." The cane seemed more accessory than aid as Bertie led them across the workshop to a table. A tarp draped across it covered an oval-shaped object less than a foot high, but twice as long and wide. Bertie pulled the tarp off to reveal the last thing Parker expected to see.

Bertie took in their reactions and loosed a deeply satisfied chuckle. "What you see is a bad decision that weighs three hundred pounds."

"*You* carved an exact replica?" Jane asked.

"Had a good model for it, in case you forgot." Thick knuckles rapped on the reproduction Stone of Scone, red sandstone with a cross carved on the top. "Thought it would be good for tourists, but I am a daft old fool. All it does is invite more questions. Damn thing would be in a lake by now if it wasn't so heavy."

"No wonder the police thought they had a fake," Parker said. "This thing looks legit to me."

Bertie smacked Parker's shin with his cane. "The authorities never accused me of stealing the Stone. I fixed it, then gave it back." He pointed to the rock. "I carved this rock after the lads came to pick up the real one."

Jane's hand skipped over the smooth stone. "Did you tell them to give it back?"

One white hedge above Bertie's eye rose. "Now, young lady, why would I do that? The English stole it from us. No reason to give it back."

"I thought you didn't care one way or the other."

"What I am is sick of this business. At the time, I had no idea what was coming." He led them back to the smaller table. "Fill your glasses," Bertie ordered. "Letting this whiskey sit out is a crime."

He sipped at his glass. "That's better. Now, about those lads and the stone." The rocking chair creaked as Bertie leaned back. "One day a car pulls up, right outside my front door. I went out to chat with the boys. Seemed nervous, but after a talk they showed me what they wanted. The boot opens, and what do I see? The Stone of bloody Scone. In my shop."

"Did they expect you not to recognize it?" Parker asked.

"Back then, not many had laid eyes on it. Being a mason, I had seen pictures once or twice, and I knew the stories. Those boys weren't thinking clearly."

Jane took a biscuit off the tea service. "Those kids never suspected you knew what it was?"

"By then they just wanted rid of it," Bertie said. "I repaired it, I got paid, they took the stone, and a week later it was left in a church." His cane thumped the ground. "Damn thing was nothing but trouble."

"Not everyone gets to touch and work with a piece of their national history," Parker said.

Bertie leaned toward him. "What would you do if a man walked into your office with the bloody United States Constitution and asked you to patch up a hole in it?" Parker opened his mouth, then closed it. "See? Not as simple as you think. Bertie Gray has been around long enough to know danger. Those kids were in it up to their necks. Best thing to do was get rid of them fast, so I fixed it up and off they went."

Parker had never really thought about it like that. A stolen treasure showed up on your doorstep, you'd be crazy not to be spooked. No telling who might come looking for it, and not in a mood to ask questions. "Are you worried about the email?" he asked. "These guys mean business, Mr. Gray. Not saying you can't handle it, but it's best to be prepared."

"I'm Bertie to my friends," he said. He nodded to his cup. "Top this off a wee bit, lad." This time his cane tapped the chair he sat on. "If any fool shows up looking for trouble, I can give it."

Parker leaned over and spotted a leather holster strapped beneath the seat supporting Gray's bony backside. The holster held a highly illegal sawed-off shotgun. "You're not messing around," Parker said. "That's a serious gun."

"And not the only one around here." The well-lined corner of Bernie's mouth twitched. "You ask Hugh. Trouble can knock on my door any time it likes. I'll be ready."

Jane had leaned over when Parker mentioned the weapon, and now her foot tapped a rapid beat on the floor, only stopping when she crossed her legs and wrapped both hands over the twitchy one. She took a deep swallow of tea. "I read rumors about the Stone in my research. One says you put a message in the repaired stone. Is that true?"

An engine fired to life outside the large garage, and one of the bay doors rumbled as it retracted toward the roof. The trio watched through the open door as a worker drove a small forklift into a parking spot, tires squealing as it twisted and turned. The driver shut off the engine, climbed out of the vehicle and then walked within feet of them, his steel-toed boots surprisingly quiet on the concrete floor, until he vanished back into the main shop building. The garage door rumbled back down into place again. All the while Bertie studied his two guests, never acknowledging his employee or Jane's question. When silence descended once more, he leaned over and selected a biscuit from the tea tray before speaking.

"You are the first person to ask me that. The authorities never asked, none of the glory-seekers ever asked, no one. I guess there are too many stories around that stone to keep straight." Crumbs tumbled onto his shirt as he chewed, Bertie brushing them away while he watched Parker watch him eat. "Is it true? Yes. I put a scrap of paper in there. Figured I could mark my work any way I like."

"Did you put a message in the replacement stone too?" Jane asked.

"No reason for that," Bertie said. "Why waste the paper?" With a scarcely concealed grunt Parker suspected was more for show than anything, Bertie levered himself off the chair and to his feet. He reached for the cane and leaned on it only after he stood up. "I hope you learned what you came for, because there is work to be done around here. Appreciate the whiskey and the company. Tell Hugh I said hello. Be nice to see him. Too many years for us both."

With that, Bertie Gray turned and left, leaving them with a half-empty whiskey bottle and more questions than answers. "Take care of yourself," Jane said. Bertie's hand came up, but he never looked back, and the door to his store closed with a soft, final click. "I guess that's it," Jane said.

"I like him," Parker said. "Crazy to keep that shotgun under his chair, but I wouldn't bet against him in a fight."

"Let's hope it never comes to that." Jane walked over to the replica Stone of Scone. "His story is amazing. And now he's sick of it after all these years." She rubbed the sandstone again, her fingers sliding across the carved cross. "He had the actual Stone here, and he didn't do anything about it. Just his job." She turned toward Parker. "Doesn't that seem odd to you? A fellow has one of Scotland's most prized artifacts come through his door, and he says nothing at all? He could have been arrested along with the thieves, but he fixes it and keeps quiet."

"Sounds to me like he didn't think stealing it from the British was so bad. Giving them what they deserved, considering they stole it first."

She punched his arm lightly. "Exactly what I thought. Bertie Gray is a Scot through and through. The last thing he wants is any Englishman telling him what to do, and I bet that applies to every Brit who ever lived. Double if they stole something from Scotland." She headed for the door. "Come on. The real Stone is right where everyone thinks it is in Edinburgh."

Out the door they went. The car's leather seat scorched Parker's arm when he got in; the air was like breathing in a furnace. "Get that air conditioning on," he said. Hot wasn't helping clear his head after the impromptu happy hour. "Bertie can hold his liquor," Parker said. "We have any water in here? I caught a nice buzz from all that whiskey."

"Check behind the seat." He reached back to find several bottles. "Good thing you've been spending time in the pubs. Building up your tolerance for our mission to Bertie's."

Parker's grin didn't reach his eyes. Too many days drowning his sorrows, when he should have been outside appreciating each moment. Take one day at a time and appreciate everything. *God, I sound like a damn AA bumper sticker.*

"Anything for the team. At least we can focus on the message now," Parker said. "Did you leave it with Hugh?" Jane nodded. "Maybe he'll have figured it out."

"Hugh knows much more about Scotland than I do," she said. "My guess is we'll find him in the library, digging for answers."

"You have enough books," Parker said. "There must be thousands in there." The library was easily his favorite room in the entire castle; he'd stood transfixed by the seemingly endless shelves.

"Over ten thousand, from what my parents say. I've never counted." Back on the motorway now, Jane pulled out her phone. "Hugh left me a voicemail." Her face lit up as she listened to it. "This is interesting," she said. "Hugh thinks he found something that helps with the last message."

"What did he find?"

"A picture. He didn't say anything else."

"Call him," Parker said. The phone beeped in that peculiar European ringtone he still wasn't used to, and continued beeping until Hugh's voicemail picked up. "Hugh, we are on the way back. Can't wait to hear about what you found. Oh, and Bertie says hello." She clicked off. "He must be outside."

"Or taking a nap," Parker said. "Nice day for it."

Jane lowered their windows, and air warmed by the afternoon

sunlight whipped through the car, tossing loose strands of his hair like tiny whips. *I'm cutting it tomorrow.* He'd let it get bad, with the hair, the scruffy beard, and the pathetic paunch creeping over his belt. Who the hell was he? Six months of his life gone in a flash, with nothing to show for it but an incredible alcohol tolerance. He mulled that over on the mostly quiet ride back, until Barnbougle Castle rose in the distance.

He was still lost in a funk when Jane rolled to a stop behind the castle. Fresh, salty air blew off the estuary waters, yet he barely noticed as he stepped out of the Land Rover. Then something caught his eye, jolting him back to the present.

The rear door was ajar.

"Jane."

"One second." She had her head buried in the back seat. "Will you grab my other—"

"Look."

"What?" She stood up, arms filled with baggage. He pointed, and her eyes narrowed. "Oh. Hugh must have forgotten to close it."

So why did the hair on his neck stand up? "Think he's out doing yardwork?" He looked around but saw no sign of Hugh anywhere. "Where would he be?"

"I'm sure everything is fine," she said, and headed for the door.

Parker trailed her inside, where the stone walls kept out the day's warmth. Cool air chilled his ankles, and his heart beat faster. Everyday creaks in the ancient house caught his ear; the wind whistled through at least one open window. Jane dropped her bags and took one of the two main staircases up to the second floor, where she stepped into the two-story library.

"Hugh, are you in here?" she called.

Parker walked in after her and found an empty room.

"He was in here today," Jane said, her brow furrowed. "The ladder has been moved."

Access to the highest shelves came from a rolling ladder mounted on the second-story walkway. "I hope he didn't fall and break his neck."

Jane laughed. "Hugh? He's been climbing those steps since before I was born. When he goes it won't be a slip of the foot that kills him." Despite this, she stood on her toes to survey the upper walkway. "Not up there. I'm sure he's outside somewhere." She pushed past him and headed for the kitchen. "How does a sandwich sound? I'm starving."

Parker's stomach rumbled at the thought. The whiskey had worn off, and right now lunch sounded terrific. "Do you have anything here to eat?"

"Do we have food?" She chuckled. "Hugh never wants to be short of provisions." She turned for the kitchen as a grandfather clock chimed the hour. "We could survive for months on what's in the larder."

"Sounds good to me." Visions of overstuffed sandwiches danced in his head, so much so that he didn't notice Jane stop until he crashed into her as they entered the massive main room on the second floor. "Sorry about that." She didn't respond, just kept staring into the room ahead. Light drifted down from the third-floor windows. Her shoulders were trembling when Parker brushed past.

Two boots stuck out from behind an end table, backlit by the dying fire crackling in the massive hearth. "That's Hugh." Parker darted around the table to find the big man sprawled face down on the floor. A trickle of blood stained the stone floor beneath him, trailing from a cut on his forehead. "Hugh?" He grabbed a thick shoulder, shaking hard. "Hugh, get up!" When the old caretaker didn't move, Parker placed both hands under him and turned him over on his back.

He put two fingers on his neck. "He's breathing, and his pulse is strong." He peered more closely. A drop of red stained Hugh's neck. "It looks like he's been cut here too. Wait a second." Parker leaned over. "It almost looks like a needle prick on—"

Behind him, Jane screamed. The clock struck again, a shoe scraped on stone, and Parker caught a glimpse of something coming at him before an anvil landed on his head. White light exploded toward the edges of his vision, the floor rushing up to meet him as the room went dark.

His feet were burning. Not burning, but roasting, cooked under a desert sun until they swelled too large for his shoes. *What's wrong with me?* Swimming through the foggy cotton of the half-conscious, Parker tried to shout, tried to pull himself awake, but nothing worked. His arms wouldn't move, his voice didn't work, and he could scarcely move his legs. He finally managed to blink. One eye cracked open; a clock hung on the wall above him. Five past the hour. *The hour rang when we got here. I've been out for five minutes.*

A firecracker burst behind him, enough to jumpstart one leg, and the other soon followed. About the time he got his arms moving, another explosion blew tiny sparks through the air. The fire, burning low and hot inches from his feet. His shoes must be close to melting. On shaky arms he pulled himself toward cooler air and things got better, at least until he sat up. Then his head felt like a bomb had gone off inside it. Pain ruled his body, but it all vanished as his memory returned.

Jane. He'd been out for five minutes, giving whoever whacked him plenty of time to hurt her. Where was she? He turned his head to the side, fighting a wave of nausea. Hugh hadn't moved. Parker reached a hand toward him and felt his neck. The old man's pulse was still strong, though he didn't so much as stir when Parker shook him. The dribble of blood on his neck had dried by now. *That definitely looks like a needle prick. Whoever did this must have drugged Hugh. Explains why he's still out cold.*

Gritting his teeth against the thunderous pain bouncing in his skull, Parker began to push himself up to a standing position, and nearly faceplanted back onto the stone. He threw his hands out to steady himself. Damn, that was his blood on the floor. He touched the back of his head and gingerly touched a nasty wound. He pulled his fingers away; they were stained red. He knew that head wounds bled a lot and tended to look – and feel – worse than they actually were. Worse had befallen his abused head, he thought ruefully, and he'd survived.

Avoiding the puddle of blood, he got up, more slowly this time, and made it to a front window on unsteady feet. A noise whispered past his ear as he reached the sill. He froze, listening. *There it is.* A long, drawn-out creak, the kind a door makes when it's been on the same hinges for generations in a chilly castle. Upstairs or down? Hard to tell, but Parker's money was on down. Moving with care, he dodged the slumbering Hugh and made for the stairs, brushing past the table where the three of them had sat together several times, and where Hugh's tobacco had spilled over a black-and-white photo. He must have been packing his pipe when the intruder came.

A bell dinged in Parker's head, so faint he nearly missed it. He went back to the table and studied the mess. *What is it?* This table meant something, was calling out to him, but damned if he knew why. He blinked, and it came to him. *The picture.* Hugh had left a message about a picture. He thought it held the answer. Could this be it?

He brushed aside the spilled tobacco to reveal a photograph of a building, all stone with a tall wooden door in the middle. Two people stood in front of the open door, a young boy and an old man. The old man looked like Hugh, thick beard and all, but judging from their clothes the photo was nearly a hundred years old. Hugh wouldn't have been more than a child when it was taken.

Another bell went off, louder this time. Parker snatched the photo. The older man did resemble Hugh after a fashion. The child, however… He had no idea. It seemed to be the right age. Was the little one Hugh as a boy? Jane had told him Hugh's family had served as caretakers of Barnbougle Castle for generations, so it *was* possible.

But why would an old picture of Hugh and his grandfather matter now? They stood in front of the castle, the front door closed behind them. Not much else in the shot, just the metal placard outside Barnbougle's front door, letting people know the castle's name and when it had been built.

He didn't have time for this. Not now. As he set the picture down, one other detail grabbed his eye. The nameplate. It wasn't *exactly* the same. An extra line of text sat between the name and date. Written in a language he didn't know.

Barnbougle Castle
Ciobair Cnoc
Circa 1201

What did it mean? He obviously couldn't ask Hugh right now.

A noise came from downstairs, another door creaking. He stuffed the photo in his pocket and crept to the staircase.

He paused at the top of the stairs. What rooms were on the first level? He'd only been to a few of them. Two long hallways ran the length of the floor, with several shorter hallways connecting the two, while staircases led up to the second level on either side.

Parker made his way silently back to the kitchen and grabbed a knife. The heavy blade offered faint reassurance: only fools brought knives to a gun fight. But it was all he had. Parker crept downstairs. *Deep breaths. Stay focused.* His heart thundered, and the walls seemed to lean toward him on both sides; his footsteps seemed too loud.

Shouting pain throbbed in his skull with each step as he made it to the lower level. The front door was to one side, sunlight spilling across the hallway to set countless dust motes alight. A shadow flashed across the glass outside. Parker moved through the closest doorway, staying below the window and out of sight. Back pressed against the wall, he stood until he could peer outside toward the driveway.

A car approached and then parked. A sedan, one he'd never seen. The driver's door opened to reveal a man, now cast in silhouette with the sun to his rear. The passenger door opened as well, and another silhouetted figure stepped out.

Only when they got closer did Parker see their faces. He sagged with relief – it wasn't Jankowski's friend from the cemetery coming to find them after all. He recognized the first one, the administrator from Jane's department, carrying a set of books. *Tom Gregan.* Why was he here? Parker needed to warn him off: if he let him walk in here, Tom could catch a bullet for his trouble.

He still couldn't see the other person.

Edging the window open, Parker whistled softly as Tom walked up the front steps. "Over here." Tom Gregan looked everywhere but at Parker. "Tom," he hissed. "Over here." The administrator spotted Parker, who held a finger to his lips. "Be quiet."

A voice he remembered cut through the still air.

"Who is speaking? Tom, who is it?" Grace Astor marched around Tom and directly toward the window. "What the devil are you after?" She squinted at Parker, and then a strange look flashed across her face. "Mr. Chase."

Tom darted in front of Grace. "What's going on?"

"Someone's in here with a gun." Tom's eyes went wide. "Do you have a phone?" Parker had left his upstairs.

"I do." He reached into his back pocket.

"Call the police. Tell them there's an armed intruder and an injured man in Jane's house."

Tom jerked back as though the words stung. "Where's Jane?"

"I think she's hiding. When we got back, we found Hugh upstairs. He's unconscious."

Grace pushed her way past Tom, who walked away with his phone pressed to his ear. "What is going on here?" she asked. "You said there is a gunman inside?"

Parker briefly recapped the recent events, from their arrival to him waking up next to Hugh, with the caretaker still out cold.

"Have you seen who did this?" she demanded.

"No. Whoever it was snuck up on us and whacked my head. I was out for five minutes. When I woke up Jane was gone, along with whoever hit me."

Tom finished his call and came back over to the window. "The authorities are coming. What did you say about Jane?" he asked. "Shouldn't I come in and help find her?" Not waiting for an answer, he slid the window open from the outside and climbed through. Parker stepped to one side to give him room, his head thumping unpleasantly as he came in.

"You are not leaving me out here," Grace said, and before Parker could react, she tossed her high heels on the ground and deftly swung herself through the window, her pantsuit legs swishing as she landed. "I will not be forgotten outside while you two are in here."

Parker may as well have argued with Queen Elizabeth. "Fine, but please be quiet. I heard noise down here. My guess is whoever's here is on this level. How long did the cops say they'd be?"

"They said they'd be here in a matter of minutes," Tom said.

"Good. When they get here, we go outside. Stay in here and there's a good chance one of us gets shot instead of the bad guy." But that didn't mean he was leaving Jane on her own. Not a chance. "Let's go find Jane."

"Did you hear anything else?" asked Tom.

"Nothing," Parker said. "This place is huge. I say we stick together and go through this level room by room."

"We can cover more ground if we split up," Tom said.

"True, but if there's only one guy here, we should go after him together."

Tom drew back. "You want to *attack* this man? He has a gun."

Grace grabbed Tom's arm. "Of course we will attack him. It is no use sitting around waiting for things to happen." Tom opened his mouth, then thought better of it.

"Are you sure you want to be in here?" Parker asked. Grace's only response was a withering glare. "Okay. I'll run interference while Tom sneaks up on him from behind." Tom was less than thrilled with the idea. "Only if it's safe," Parker assured him. "Relatively speaking. At the very least we can figure out where he is and tell the cops." He flashed the knife in his hand. "Stay with me. If it goes bad, both of you run for it and get outside. I'll hold him off so you can warn the police about what's going on."

"A knife is not ideal against a gun," Tom said. "I suggest we try to find him before doing anything rash."

Sound advice, which Parker had no intention of taking. "I'll be careful. Now try not to make any noise." Parker stuck his head out and looked both ways before going into the hallway. The problem with this place wasn't just the size, but the number of rooms. Any number of intruders could be spread across multiple rooms searching for Jane – if she hadn't been caught already. But she was smart, and this was her home.

The trio crept down the hall in silence, stopping outside a half-open door as Parker peered through. He didn't hear anything except his own heartbeat, so he waited, letting his eyes play back and forth over the room. No one jumped out, no arms twitched, no shoulders moved in the shadows.

"Stay here," Parker whispered to Tom and Grace. "If I get shot, run outside and don't stop until you find the police." With that, he slipped into the room.

It proved empty, including the closets, so Parker moved to the next room. Again he waited, watched and listened before entering, and again found no madmen with guns. The third room proved equally empty. As he sidled toward the next in line, Tom and Grace tiptoeing behind him, a drawn-out creak stopped him in his tracks.

"Near the back staircase," Tom whispered, pointing over Parker's shoulder.

Parker glanced behind him. Those stairs led up to the kitchen.

"Wait here," he said. "No one's behind you. It's a clear exit if you need to get out." He turned to Grace. "Please stay with Tom," he whispered. She gave him a haughty look but stayed put.

"We will come to you if I hear anything," Tom said.

"Don't sneak up on me." Parker nodded to the knife. "Wouldn't want to stab you by mistake." He grinned at the administrator's suddenly colorless cheeks. "Just kidding. But seriously, let me know you're there."

Tom didn't smile. "I will."

Parker crept to the rear stairway, pausing only to glance inside each room for movement. A breeze touched his cheek, the air warm and fragrant even as it blew in off the water through the still-open back door. *Maybe the wind is blowing these doors around.* Had the intruder already made off with Jane and he was wasting his time? Every minute counted now. A cold hand seized Parker's chest, squeezing softly at first, then tighter with each breath. Nothing moved outside but the tall grass, stems swaying in the wind. The mausoleum jutted up near the water's edge. Not a person in sight. Parker turned back toward Tom and Grace, glancing up the steps as he did.

A person's shadow slid across the wall above him.

Way too big to be Jane's. He blinked and it vanished, headed toward where Hugh was lying unconscious. Parker flashed one finger at Tom and pointed upstairs, mouthing *Somebody is up there.*

Tom nodded, pointing back over his shoulder toward the other staircase located by the front entrance, and indicating that he and Grace would go up one while Parker went up the other. They didn't wait for Parker to disagree, hurrying down the hall and out of sight up the stairs before Parker could stop them. *Idiots.* Going up there unarmed, and the guy had a gun.

Too late now. Maybe Parker could distract the intruder, give Tom a chance to overpower him. Or maybe there were two armed men up there waiting to gun them down. But if that was the case, why did he have a nasty welt on his head? If whoever did that wanted him dead, they'd have shot him.

Too many variables. That's what it came back to. One fact in all the uncertainty was that Jane needed help, and only three people were around to provide it, so he headed up the stairs toward an unknown adversary, ignoring the small voice screaming in the back of his mind that this was a bad idea. The kind of idea people had right before they got shot.

The voice in his head vanished when he reached the top. *Show time.* He leaned around the corner, his head at ground level. The man whose shadow had covered the wall moments ago was on the move, halfway across the massive main room with his back to Parker. He passed a still-unconscious Hugh and headed for the steps leading upstairs to the third level, a pistol leading the way. His path wouldn't cross the far staircase, the one Tom and Grace had taken. Still no sign of Jane – had she run up to the third level?

The man stopped halfway up the stairs and reached into his pocket. Out came a cell phone, and he turned as he studied it, bringing his face in profile. Parker squinted. It was the second man from the graveyard, Jankowski's partner. *Great.* Chances were this guy knew Jankowski was dead, and he knew Parker had played a part in it. So why let him live earlier? It made no sense, unless he needed Parker alive.

The man continued up the stairs, moving with assurance now, until the ceiling seemed to swallow him whole. Parker tiptoed from his hiding spot and ran to a table, ducking behind it and craning his neck for a glimpse of the gunman without success. No way to see what he was doing without going to the next floor. And what had happened to the other two?

After confirming that Hugh was still breathing, Parker crept past the still-crackling fire, keeping as close to the wall as possible. The burning wood briefly warmed his back, and then his fingers played over the wall medallion, the Saint Andrew's Cross hiding a secret passageway to the basement.

No time for that now. He crept toward the other stairwell leading up from the first level and nearly fell over Tom and Grace, who were pressed against the wall at the top step. Tom nearly tumbled back down before he grabbed the handrail. Grace barely budged.

"Christ's blood, you scared me." Tom let out a long breath. "I did not expect to see you."

"Keep it down. The guy's armed, and I've seen him before." Tom frowned. "I'll explain later," Parker said. "He went to the top floor. I think Jane's up there."

"What if she got away?"

"Then why is this guy still here? He's not looking for anything, not from what I saw. He's trying to be quiet. Makes me think Jane's still here and he can't find her." He grabbed Tom's arm and pulled him across to the kitchen. "Take this," he said, handing Tom a knife. "It's better than nothing."

"I'll take that." Grace snatched the blade. "Tom can find his own."

"I do not want to stab anyone," Tom said.

"Say that when he's about to shoot you and I'll believe it. You wanted to come inside, remember?"

"That's not a problem for me." Grace jabbed the knife toward Parker. "Now get going. Tom and I will watch your back."

At least one of them had a spine. "Don't make a move unless you can get the drop on him. Wouldn't want either of you to get shot."

"What do you propose we do?" Tom asked.

A good question. There was at least one gunman upstairs. Likely just the one, mainly because they hadn't run into anybody else. Assuming that, the three of them outnumbered this guy – and they had one other advantage. "He doesn't know we're here," Parker said. "If we can catch him off guard, we can take him down without anyone getting shot."

"He can fire the gun quickly," Tom said.

"Then don't mess around. I'll distract him, and you two come from behind." He frowned. "Except we have no idea where he is. Never mind." If he was certain Jane wasn't trapped up there, they could simply go outside and wait for the police to arrive. But if Jane was up there, they didn't have time to wait. "I'll go up. Wait here. I'll be back in a second."

"We can watch for the police," Tom said, indicating a window. "Tell them what we know when they arrive." He clapped a hand on Parker's shoulder. "Be careful." Grace didn't offer any advice, instead only waving toward the staircase with her knife.

Parker walked over one heavy rug and then another, moving at right angles to the staircase. It took longer, but he stayed mostly out of view and deadened his footsteps to nothing. Air whistled around closed windows as he set his foot on the first step; he looked back to find Tom and Grace had vanished. *Smart move.* If they had gone outside, they could tell the cops what was going on once they arrived.

He turned his attention back to the steps. Even though they had no runner, they were solid stone and gave off practically zero noise as he climbed. A fly buzzed past his ear. *Think, Parker. How is the upper floor laid out?* The building was a rectangle, though the staircase up which the gunman had traveled led to a walkway, which mirrored the exterior. Thick walls and sturdy construction served to silence his approach – and would do the same for the intruder. The guy could be hiding around the next corner and Parker wouldn't know it. Either that, or he was searching for Jane right now. *If he's looking for her, I can get the drop on him.*

He held onto the wooden guiderail, polished wood gleaming as sunlight fell over it. One more step and he would be able to see into the third level, down both sides of the upper walkway. As he took the next step, a thought strafed his mind.

Why didn't he react when he realized I was gone?

The last time this guy had seen Parker, he'd been out cold next to Hugh. In his haste to help Jane, Parker had never even considered this angle. A missing body should have startled the man and set him searching. Now the guy had two people running around and no clue where either was, but he wasn't even reacting. He'd walked right past where Parker had fallen, pulled his phone out, and then kept moving. Why?

The light changed as a cloud covered the sun for an instant.

Wait a second. There wasn't a cloud in the sky. A sea of blue had stretched to infinity as he and Jane had driven back from Bertie Gray's shop. She'd commented on how pretty the view was. *Those aren't clouds moving.*

The intruder's head appeared to Parker's right, his strangely calm face behind bars as he moved past the handrail posts.

Parker whipped his knife between two posts at the same instant the man spotted him. The guy twisted, deflecting the knife with his upper arm. A wicked gash opened along one bicep and the man let out a muffled curse. Parker ran back down the stairs and dashed for the study as a gunshot boomed off the stone walls.

At least he's not chasing Jane now. Feet pounded the staircase he'd just run down as the gunman gave chase. Without a firearm, Parker knew his best chance lay in using the castle's many rooms and levels to his advantage. Parker kept one eye open for Tom and Grace, but they'd vanished. *You two are on your own for now.* Parker darted toward the far stairway, grabbing another knife from the kitchen as he cast a rueful glance toward Hugh's prone figure. A gunshot boomed, the bullet whizzing well high to explode off a stone wall as Parker made it to the staircase and ran down to the first level. He headed straight for the Saint Andrew's Cross medallion.

Praying that Hugh had kept the hinges oiled, he twisted the medallion and the door silently slid open as he heard the sound of footsteps coming downstairs. Parker darted into the tunnel and pulled the door quietly shut; darkness enveloped him. This corridor might as well have been an underground tomb.

Gooseflesh rose on his arms and neck in the cool confines. The darkness was oppressive, but he was finally taking charge, taking it to the gunman. Nobody else knew these corridors existed. Reaching for the light switch, he stopped. *Jane knew.* Could she have hidden in here? Bulbs flashed to life overhead, and light flooded the passage.

Stairs rose ahead, leading straight up to a landing before switching back. He hurried up to the landing and craned his neck. "Jane?" The tunnel swallowed his whispers. "It's Parker," he said, a bit louder. "Are you up there?" No response. Running to the second level, he pressed an ear to the exit door and waited. Nothing came through What would the intruder think? Parker had run downstairs and vanished into thin air. If he were the one giving chase, he'd think Parker had doubled back, using the other staircase to head back upstairs. Parker turned and ran back down to the first level door and pressed his ear to it.

Another deep breath. As he listened for any noise, hope blossomed in his chest. Jane might not be in this passage, but what about the other one? Maybe she'd secreted herself in the second passage, the one leading from the library to the master bedroom.

Or maybe not. Again, too many variables at play to stay put. Tom and Grace were out there, a man ill-equipped for this kind of thing and a feisty, undersized lady. Not that Parker was a pro, but he couldn't leave them to their fate. They needed help, and fast. But how?

A muffled creak caught his ear, like a door opening and closing on the breeze. Except this time the creak ended in a thud. Now he definitely heard footsteps, moving past the hidden door and then fading to nothing. Unless Tom and Grace were slamming doors, the gunman was still on the first level, but had moved out of hearing range. Time to go. Without giving himself a chance to rethink it, Parker flicked off the lights and twisted the Saint Andrews Cross medallion on the inside of the hidden door in front of him. The door yawned open.

A first-level hallway was outside. Most importantly, no intruder waited.

Orange sunlight spilled across the hall floor as he stepped out, at the same time someone else stepped out of a doorway down the hall. He tensed and nearly threw his knife before he realized the intruder wasn't facing him. And where was the flat cap he'd been wearing?

Parker narrowed his gaze. *Tom.*

"Hey." Parker jumped back as Tom twisted around, knife at the ready. "Easy," he whispered. "It's me."

"Parker?" Tom put his weapon down. "Where did you go? I searched every room down here."

Grace darted into the hallway as they spoke. "What did you see?"

"I ran across the intruder, but he's still out there." He cut Grace off before she could continue. "Did you find Jane?"

Tom glanced at Grace. "We did not." He pointed to the ceiling. "The other man is up there. I heard him walking around."

"That could be a problem," Parker said. "I think Jane is up there."

"How could you possibly know that?" Grace asked.

"I'll show you. Stay with me and don't make any noise." The pair fell in step behind him as they headed upstairs, occasional muffled noises floating downstairs, though nothing clear. The intruder could be anywhere up there. "We're going to the library," he told them.

Grace pushed past Tom. "Is Jane hiding in there?" she asked.

"Maybe."

They made it up to the second level and ran directly into the cavernous library without glimpsing the intruder. "Stay here." Parker posted Tom at the door, not bothering to stop Grace from following. "If you hear him coming, run over to me."

"But we will be trapped."

Parker winked. "Trust me on this."

Leaving Tom and Grace standing watch, Parker followed the book-lined walls around the room's circumference. He nearly missed the medallion, attached to a support beam and almost invisible among the colorful book spines. The Saint Andrew's Cross twisted, a hidden counterweight moved, and a portion of shelving swung out toward Parker. He stepped back and found Jane leaning against the frame, arms crossed on her chest.

"What took you so long?"

"How'd you know it was me? And I'm fine, in case you're wondering."

Jane jumped out and wrapped him in a fierce embrace. "You and Hugh are the only people who know about this passage." She tensed in his arms. "Who is – *Tom*?" She pushed Parker away. "What are – *Grace*?" Jane's eyes went wide. "Why are you two here?"

"A hidden door?" Tom slipped his phone away and hurried over, walking right past Jane as he went to the false shelves. "How intriguing. You have a secret room behind the wall?"

"What are you doing here?" she asked.

"I came to deliver a package," Tom said. "It was marked URGENT, and since you were on the road, I decided a trip was in order. Grace was visiting the school and decided to join me."

"I wanted an update on your research," Grace said. Sunlight sparked off one of her rings. "This is not what I expected."

"You two should have stayed there," Jane said, then turned to Parker. "Is the intruder still here?"

"We heard him upstairs. Come on, let's get out of here." Parker twisted the medallion, and the door nearly clipped Tom as it closed. Everyone followed Parker to the library door, where he leaned out, listening. "I can't hear him." A cross-breeze followed them to the closest staircase, carrying scents of wildflowers and summer grass. No sound of the intruder. Or of police sirens, for that matter.

The group hurried to the nearby staircase and went down, Parker first, stopping at the bottom step to check the hallway. Nothing. Jane stood beside him and pointed toward the front exit.

"Closer to the police," she said, her breath warm on his ear. He nodded. The police would get here, arrest the intruder, and they could put all this behind them. Hopefully Jane would agree this was enough excitement for one artifact. Whatever James and Philip had hidden could stay lost now, for all he cared. Nothing was worth dying over.

Sunlight sparkled on the glass in the front door, a prism of every color marking their final escape.

Parker reached for the doorknob and the intruder stepped out of a room beside it, staring from under his flat cap with vacant eyes. He pointed his gun at Parker's chest.

"Don't move."

Chapter 12

Barnbougle Castle

Parker brandished his knife, but the intruder darted out of range.

"Drop it," he said in a thick brogue. "On the floor." A torn strip of fabric adorned the man's upper arm, stained dark over the wound.

Parker stepped in front of Jane as he tossed the knife aside. "What do you want?"

The man ignored him, pointing the gun at Grace. "You, drop the knife." Her eyes narrowed, then she tossed it near his feet. "Upstairs." He flicked the gun. "Now."

Parker took another step back toward Jane, and then she whispered in his ear. "Duck." Parker hit the deck as a knife buzzed past his head toward the gunman. Flipping end over end, it slammed into his face handle first, knocking his cap off and sending him stumbling back and his pistol flying.

Parker shoved Jane toward the stairs. "Go," he shouted. She bounced off Tom and knocked him back, while Grace scurried off in the opposite direction, sliding past the gunman as he bent over to retrieve his firearm and out of sight with surprising speed. After making sure Jane was out of harm's way, Parker took a step toward the intruder, but it was too late. The guy was reaching for his weapon and Parker was too far away. Instead of attacking, Parker raced up the stairs, cruising past Jane and Tom. Once the gunman got upstairs, the hallway would be a shooting gallery. Time to get into the secret passageway. The police had to be close by now, so they only needed to hold on a little longer. Parker cleared the top step and ran toward the hidden door, and his heart dropped when Jane screamed.

"Let go of me," she shouted. "Tom, what's wrong with you? Let me go!" A hand appeared at the bottom of the steps. Jane's hand, scrabbling for purchase. Her brunette hair flew wildly about. "Stop it!" Then she vanished.

What the hell is he doing? Parker took one step back down the stairs before the gunman appeared, holding his face with the injured arm and waving his pistol with the other. Blood poured from his nose. Fighting every instinct to charge, Parker ran into the study, where he twisted the Saint Andrew's Cross. The door opened and Parker jumped inside. It swung noiselessly shut as the gunman burst into the study.

Parker leaned against the wall in the pitch blackness, struggling to catch his breath. So that's why their antagonists had followed their every move. They had a traitor in their midst: Tom Gregan.

How long had he been selling them out? He had all the access necessary to keep tabs on them from his office, sharing their plans and findings with whoever employed the two graveyard thugs, willing to kill for the hidden letter, for whatever waited at the end of James's path. No wonder he and Jane hadn't been able to lose their pursuers. They had known where Jane and Parker were going every time. He took a deep breath as the noises outside faded. Flat-cap had moved on.

The cold shock in his gut dissipated, replaced with roiling anger and an energy Parker hadn't felt in months. So Tom Gregan wanted to mess with Parker, was willing to attack Hugh to get at Jane's information? Well, he and Flat-cap now had a problem on their hands, and no idea where it was coming from. Tom didn't know about this second hidden passage.

Parker slipped through the dark, feeling his way downstairs. No reason to risk turning the lights on now. Standing in front of the bottom door, Parker reached for the interior medallion, but then stopped. Flat-cap had a gun. Parker didn't even have a knife, and the only thing worse than bringing a knife to a gun fight was bringing nothing at all. Maybe he should wait for the police.

The police Tom called. Damn. That's why they hadn't arrived. Tom had never called. Parker, Jane and Grace Astor, who was hopefully outside and away from here by now, were alone out here and practically unarmed. Hell, he might as well grab a flaming log from the fireplace and throw it at them.

He blinked. The fireplace. That was *exactly* what he needed. Parker ran back upstairs and leaned an ear against the hidden door there, listening for silence and finding it. With a deep breath, he twisted the medallion, ready to drop and roll if bullets started flying.

They didn't. Blinking furiously in the bright light, Parker slipped out, closed the door, and hurried to the fireplace, where Jane's father's hunting rifle waited above the dying fire. *Score one for the good guys.* He lifted the gun from its perch. It had recently been cleaned by Hugh and was ready for action, the wood polished yet worn, the metal smooth.

Don't worry, Hugh. I'll get him for you. Hugh had even had the foresight to leave a box of ammunition on the mantel, and Parker loaded the weapon. He pocketed the rest of the cartridges and went to the nearest staircase, ducking down as he heard a voice coming from one of the open windows. Was Flat-cap outside? He slipped toward the window and knelt beneath it. There it was again, louder this time. He glanced outside and saw Flat-cap standing in the yard below with a phone held to his ear.

"Nobody out here, boss," Flat-cap said. "I'm coming inside." The man disappeared from view and a door slammed shut. *He's right below me.* Parker flicked the gun's safety off. If Flat-cap walked down the hallway, he'd cross the mouth of the stairwell, giving Parker a shot. Of course, even wide-open shots sometimes went wrong.

He went to one knee and took several deep breaths, settling into the familiar routine. *Stay calm. Breathe easy.* He closed one eye and waited for his target. Footsteps sounded down the hallway, and Parker's finger tightened on the trigger.

A scream sliced through the castle. *Jane.*

Flat-cap stopped at the stairway's edge. Parker squeezed, the rifle boomed, and Jane's scream died halfway through. Years of training took over, years spent in the wild hunting, and Parker didn't react. He pulled the bolt back and slammed a new round home. The pistol went off again and again as Flat-cap fired wildly up the stairs; none of the shots came anywhere near him. Parker fired again and Flat-cap twisted to the ground. Parker reloaded and fired one last time, hitting Flat-cap center chest and sending him down for good.

A pistol shot cracked the air and Parker's rifle jerked from his grasp, sending him onto his backside. Tom stood across the second floor at the top of the other staircase. He fired again and missed. Parker dove behind a table, flipping it down in front of him as he scrambled for cover.

Flat-cap must have given Tom a gun, but he clearly had no idea how to handle it. A kid could shoot better than him. A bullet ripped through the upended table, leaving a smoking hole inches from his head. *Damn. He doesn't have to be good. Lucky counts too.*

Think, think. Flat-cap had had a gun when Parker shot him, a gun that should be at the bottom of the stairs by his corpse. Scrambling into a crouch, Parker stuck a hand to one side and waved, away from the stairs. Tom obliged by firing.

Parker dove for the nearby staircase and Tom kept firing as he landed on the steps, knocking the wind from his gut. He scrambled downstairs and tumbled out at the bottom, scraped and bleeding as he landed on Flat-cap's corpse. *Where was the gun?* Tom appeared at the top of the stairs. Parker rolled aside as a bullet exploded by his head. Footsteps pounded down the stairs. Parker stood, and then he saw her.

Jane. Lying on the floor, blood covering her face. *Oh God, no.*

"Do not move!"

Parker moved toward Jane, but stopped when Tom fired. The bullet hit the floor in front of him and Parker backed up. Tom came down the stairs and started toward him, the gun held out in front.

"Stop this!" Tom's chest heaved. "You made me do this." He stopped, the gun wobbling slightly. "It is your fault."

"What are you talking about?" Parker asked. He stepped back, bumped into a chair near the front door. If he kept Tom talking, he could throw it at him, maybe knock him down.

"It is your fault," Tom said again. "Your fault. Your fault." He repeated it almost mechanically, not listening to anything Parker said. The guy was in shock, either at what he'd done or from blood loss, Parker didn't know. "This is because of you."

Parker opened his mouth to protest, but Tom suddenly went still.

"I expect we are both sorry for this." He pointed the gun at Parker's chest and pulled the trigger.

Which fell on an empty chamber. *Six shots. He'd fired six times.* The cylinder was empty.

With a grunt of rage, Tom threw his gun at Parker and lunged for Flat-cap's weapon. He nearly had it when Parker spotted a glint of something metal on the floor. *A knife.* Jane's knife. He grabbed it and turned back to Tom.

Tom snatched up Flat-cap's gun at the same time as Parker launched himself through the air. Fire burst from the barrel as Parker's full weight crashed into Tom's chest. The gunshot sounded like cannon fire next to his ear. He and Tom tumbled back against the wall together, and the shot went wide. Parker scrambled to his feet and turned to see Tom up on one elbow, leveling Flat-cap's gun at him and then glancing up the stairs. A smile crossed his lips.

"We—"

A gun went off. Parker ducked as it fired again, belatedly realizing Tom didn't have any bullets. *Then who was shooting?*

He glanced back at Tom, who was sprawled on the floor, his body limp. Blood ran from a wound in his forehead. Grace Astor walked down the staircase with a small pistol held in front of her, the barrel trained on Tom.

"The threat has been eliminated, Mr. Chase." She pointed the pistol at him as he stumbled straight for Jane, then froze. "Oh, forgive me." She looked down at Jane and lowered the weapon. "I apologize."

"No need," Parker said, covering the last few yards to kneel beside Jane. "You saved us." He grabbed Jane's shoulder. "Can you hear me?"

He touched her neck. *She's alive.* Strong pulse, steady breathing, and a wicked gash right below the hairline from where Tom must have hit her. That's why she'd stopped screaming earlier.

"Jane, get up." He shook her, softly at first, then harder. A thought struck him, and he turned to Grace. "Where did you get a gun?"

"In my car," she said. "I retrieved it a minute ago."

Why didn't you mention that before? He opened his mouth to ask, but then Jane's eyes fluttered and opened. "Parker?" She blinked and sat bolt upright. "Oh, my goodness. Where is Tom? He's working with that man." She tried to get up, only to fall on her backside. "My head. Where's Tom?"

"Dead." He pointed to the corpse. "He tried to kill me. Grace got him first."

She took in Grace, who was standing over Tom's body, then looked around wildly. "What about the other one? Where is he?"

"Also dead." Parker explained about using her father's rifle to finish off Flat-cap.

"I see." She rose, slowly this time, using the wall for support. "Are you okay?" She reached for his face. "Did you get burned?"

"Only a close call." Tom's last shot had missed, though the powder had burned hot enough to singe his eyebrows. "Don't worry about me. I've been through worse." He reached for her head. "What about you? That's a nasty cut."

"Tom hit me when I started screaming. They were planning to surround you."

"I heard you. It saved my life."

Instead of the fear he expected, her eyes narrowed and Jane stomped her foot. "That bastard. After all the years we worked together, he tries to steal my work, to *kill* me. I couldn't believe it when he grabbed me on the stairs."

"Did he say why he did it?"

"No. He kept telling me to be quiet." Her voice got soft. "They were after the messages."

"It doesn't make sense," Parker said. "We have no idea what they're talking about in those messages, and all of a sudden it's worth killing for? Not just that, but how does it all tie in with the Stone of Scone?"

"I don't know." Jane looked up at him. "Why did they come here and attack Hugh? He had nothing to do with it."

"Certain people will do anything to find what they consider treasure," Grace said. "No one knows what is at the end of the path you are following."

"Wait a second." Parker reached into his pocket. "This might help. I found it on the table where Hugh was researching." He held out the black-and-white photograph.

Jane took it and examined it, frowning, while Grace crowded over her shoulder to look. "This makes no sense," Jane said. "That's Hugh as a boy, with his grandfather. One of the first caretakers."

Parker pointed to the nameplate. "It's different. The one outside now only has words in English. I'm not sure what language it is, but there's a third line on the plate, between the English name and the date."

"It's the name of our house in Gaelic. *Ciobair Cnoc.* It translates to…" Her voice trailed off.

"To what?"

"To *shepherd's hill.*" The photo crackled. "Oh my. I never connected it."

"Connected what?" Grace asked.

"Do you think it relates to the last message we found?" Parker asked.

"I have to look." She raced upstairs, Parker and Grace close on her tail. He brought the pistol with him just in case, and a moment later they were in the study again, where Hugh lay still out cold.

"Where did you find the picture?" Jane asked when they were all upstairs.

"On the table." They stopped beside Hugh's inert frame. "I'm going to call the police," Parker said, bending down to him. "He needs an ambulance."

"He seems to be breathing well," Jane said, crouching beside him. She looked at Parker, her brow furrowed. "This has gone on long enough. Hugh's hurt, and too many people have died. We're finishing it now."

"I agree," Grace said.

Music to Parker's ears. "The picture was on top of this dictionary." Parker tapped the open book, then realized it wasn't the only open volume on the table. "And this other one. I didn't notice it."

Jane slid the dictionary aside to reveal a book of stories opened to a full-page drawing of a lone dog on a grassy landscape with water in the background, the moon overhead. The dog's head was thrown back, jaws open toward the sky. "It's a story," Parker said.

"Not quite. This one is a poem." Her lips moved silently as she read. "Not one I've ever read before. It's called *Sir Roger Mowbray.*" She flipped the page. "Look at this. The next page is dog-eared."

"The rest of the book is in perfect condition." His shoulder brushed Jane's as they read the final stanzas. "Here." He stabbed the page. "That's your castle."

Jane read the last lines aloud.

And ever when Barnbougle's lords
Are parting this scene below
Come hound and ghost to this haunted coast
With death notes winding slow.

"It's saying that whenever the Lord of Barnbougle is about to die, a ghost and hound appear. The ghost blows on his bugle, and the hound cries at the sky." She jumped up and ran off, returning a moment later holding James's last message. "Read this again and tell me what you think."

The outside world fell away as Parker skimmed the page.

"I have lost those who seek these honours. I know of a safe place for storage, where you will find them waiting should I not return. Visit the house on shepherd's hill, where the hound and horn announce death's arrival. Below ground, by S.W. and the water, you will find everything."

"The house must be this castle," Parker said. "He mentions this hound and horn myth about the owner dying, and there's water right outside." He pointed out the window. "Do you have any secret rooms underground?"

"No secret ones. Only what you can see – the mausoleum, which leads to our family burial vaults."

"How long has it been there?" Grace asked.

"The oldest grave is from 1520."

"It was here when James and Philip were alive," Parker said. "Could James have gotten in there?"

Jane shrugged. "I don't see why not. Nobody posts guards at a mausoleum."

"Anybody with the initials *S.W.* down there?"

Jane smiled for the first time since they'd returned from Glasgow. "Let's go find out."

She ran to one of their many storage rooms and grabbed flashlights, a hammer, an aerosol can and a key before leading them to the mausoleum door. The exterior portion resembled a rectangular stone tool shed with decorations beneath the gabled roof. Cooler air blew off the water, and they heard the soft sound of the lake lapping at the shoreline, while overhead nothing but blue stretched to the horizon.

"Hold these," she ordered. Parker tucked the pistol into his waistband as he took the flashlights and hammer. "I have to spray the lock. It gets tough to open with all the rain."

The lock put up a fight, though she managed to twist the oversized skeleton key with some effort, metal squealing as the door opened in fits and spurts.

"Does anyone ever go in here?" Parker asked.

"Yes, but not all of them come out," she said. "Bad joke, I know. My father never tires of telling it." She flicked a flashlight on, the darkness beyond the mausoleum door swallowing the beam at once. "Watch your heads. The ceiling is low."

"An appropriate place to keep ancient secrets," Grace said. "Or new ones."

With that she followed Jane into the cool air, then Parker ducked and brought up the rear. He reached back and touched the pistol at the small of his back, the cold steel reassuring in this dark, chilly space. Jane walked toward the lower levels.

"No one is buried up here. This room is for prayer or reflection, I suppose. Not exactly where I would do anything of the sort, but it's here." Parker trailed behind as they descended the steep stairs. "It's a tight fit down here. Watch your elbows too, or you could knock one of my ancestors on to the ground."

"Very funny."

"You'll see."

She had to be kidding. He'd never been in one of these things before. It wasn't as though they just left bodies lying out in the open. Or so he hoped.

Damp air filled his nose and lungs, the musty cold making him cough. A series of openings cut in the rock wall stretched ahead on either side.

"These are the more recent graves," Jane said. Coffins stretched out from the depths, their ends marked with the inhabitants' names and relevant dates. "Keep moving," Jane said as Parker and Grace studied the dates. "Most of these people died after 1900."

"If you were hiding a piece of paper in here, or whatever these *honours* are, where would you put it?" Parker asked.

"In the oldest tomb, far in the back. You can likely guess how often people go back there."

"Hopefully never, if they're sane. It's not as though you actually knew these people."

"I've only been in here a few times in my entire life. Nothing but bones and dust are down here now. Other than Hugh checking for leaks, nobody ever went to the oldest graves."

"Did Hugh ever mention finding anything strange?" Grace asked.

"Not that I recall," Jane said. "Hopefully we do."

The rough-hewn walls were cold to Parker's touch as they walked on, dry and dusty despite the lake right outside. Passing a thicker support pillar, he nearly ran into Jane when she stopped without warning. "Look at this," she said. "Seamus White. Died 1705."

"That's the right timeframe." He leaned down and rubbed dust from the dates.

Grace hovered over his shoulder. "Pull the coffin out," she said.

Parker looked to Jane, who nodded and grabbed one side of the wooden box. Parker did likewise. It came out with ease, clattering to the floor without much sound.

"Use the hammer to open it," Jane said.

He jammed the pointy end between the top and sides, levering it back and forth. The old wood split almost at once. Parker managed to get the lid off in two pieces and then Jane flashed her light across a macabre scene.

"Bones." She gently moved the white sticks aside, big and small bones the color of cue balls. "And cloth. Seamus's clothes are mostly dust by now."

"Do you see anything else?" Grace asked. She nudged Jane aside. "I do not."

"No. This isn't the right one." Jane set the broken lid in with the bones. "Sorry, Grandpa Seamus. I hope you don't mind."

Parker pushed the coffin back in to its slot. They searched the next three rows without any luck. As they walked, Parker kept glancing to either side, fighting off the sensation of walls closing in. No way the burial chamber narrowed to a point. It made no sense. He hurried up to stand by Jane's side.

And realized they had reached the end. "This is the last section," she said. A smooth, unmarked wall of rough stone blocked their path. "Parker, you take one side. I'll take the other. Grace, double-check our work. If we don't find anything, we'll check them all again."

Grace didn't argue, so Parker checked the top first. Three holes in each row, three rows high. Nine of Jane's ancestors had been laid to rest here. The first one he checked had died in 1538. All in the top row were old enough, but none had the right initials. Same with the second row. He knelt and promptly banged into Jane's backside, throwing him off balance and into one of the coffins at ground level. A dust cloud erupted, choking the air from his nose as grit coated his tongue.

"Sorry about that," Jane said. "Find anything?"

Parker sneezed. "Not yet." Another sneeze. "You?"

"Nothing."

"Do not give up hope," Grace said. "It *must* be here."

Parker sneezed again, which managed to both clear his nose and blow away the dust covering the nameplate inches from his face.

Stephen White B. 1471 D. 1509

Parker couldn't do anything but cough.

"Are you okay?" Jane patted his back. "Here, get up." She grabbed his shoulder, but he shrugged her off.

"Look," he finally croaked. "This one. It matches."

Grace shoved him aside. "It does. Oh my, it does. Quick, get it open."

Parker and Jane hauled the coffin out, heedless of damage this time. Parker's heart pulsed inside his eardrums as he tore Stephen White's eternal resting box to splinters.

"Sorry, Stephen."

The coffin opened to reveal a neat pile of stacked bones in one end of the box and a pile of cloth, presumably Stephen's burial shroud, wadded up in the other.

"Why are they piled up like that?" Grace asked, gesturing to the bones. The other corpse had been laid out roughly like a human lying down.

"I don't know," Jane said.

Parker reached for the clump of ancient cloth. "There are more bones in here." *Or not.* This was unlike any bones he'd ever felt. "Wait a second. These aren't bones." He pulled the cloth away.

Brilliant light of every color erupted in the crypt, coloring the walls and dancing across the floor. "What is this?" he asked.

Jane ripped the rest of the cloth away. "It's a *sword.* With a gem on the hilt. And it's made of gold." Gingerly, she lifted the rusted metal blade out of the box; it was attached to a thick, golden hilt with a stunning gem at the bottom. "What in the world is this doing in here?"

"Was he buried with it?" Parker asked.

"Not likely. A sword like this would be passed on."

Grace couldn't seem to take her eyes off the piece, reaching over to touch the hilt.

"Is there anything else in there?" Parker asked.

Jane shoved the gleaming sword at him, hilt-first. "Hold this." Damn, it was *heavy.* Stephen White must have been one strong guy. Jane fished among the cloth again. "There's more." A dull gold stick flashed under her light. "There's something on the end of this one too." A clear and polished gemstone prismed the light again, as though a disco ball twirled in the dank tomb. "Is this a walking stick?"

"For a midget, maybe," Parker said. "It looks ceremonial."

"It's a scepter," Grace said. "Look at the decoration." She ran her flashlight up and down the length.

Jane nodded. "She's right, but I have no idea what this is for. It certainly is not part of any family history I've ever heard."

While Jane and Grace fussed with the scepter, Parker aimed his light into the coffin. "Hey." Neither woman responded. "Guys, you should see this."

"This is simply amazing," Grace said without looking up. "The filigree on this handle is spectacular."

"There's something else in here."

"What? Hold this," Jane said, actually tossing the scepter at Grace. As the older woman deftly snatched it out of mid-air, Jane removed the final bit of cloth from her ancestor's grave. Red and purple light filled the air.

Parker nearly dropped his flashlight. "Holy shit. Is that—"

"A *crown*." From within the dank confines of a coffin closed five centuries ago came a crown worthy of Queen Elizabeth. Dozens of pearls dotted the golden headpiece, with green, black and pink stones alongside golden fleurs-de-lis adorning the rim. Grace opened her mouth and started to speak, but her voice trailed off.

"What did you say?" Parker asked.

"Honours," Grace said, eyes wide in the darkness. "He took them."

"I get it," Jane said, her words breathless. "The *honours*." She pointed to the unimaginable wealth lying before them. "We found them. This is what James was talking about. He stole the honours of Scotland."

"The *what?*"

Jane wasn't listening. "Parker, this changes everything. They were supposed to have been lost after 1707. They were actually in

Edinburgh Castle until 1818, but no one knew." Jane finally looked up at him. "But this can't be. They're on display in the Crown Room at Edinburgh Castle. I've seen them. Unless the government lied about it and they never actually found them."

Parker grabbed her shoulder. "You're not making any sense."

"The Honours of Scotland were lost in 1707 and then supposedly found again in 1818 and eventually returned to Edinburgh Castle. That's what every history book says." Her hands spread out over the bejeweled items between them. "Except that's impossible, because they're here. James must have stolen these and hidden them in here, in this crypt." She shook her head. "They've been buried in my yard for over three hundred years."

As Jane spoke, Grace set the scepter down and reached into a pocket. The scepter rolled toward Parker's foot, bumping gently against it.

"Careful with that thing," he said, bending to retrieve it.

Grace didn't respond, and as she took a step toward him, hand still in her pocket, the faint wail of approaching sirens filtered into the mausoleum. Grace stopped moving. For an instant something flashed across her face, a look Parker had never seen before. He blinked, and it was gone. *What the heck was that?* For a heartbeat, Grace had looked *enraged*.

She smiled now and pulled her empty hand from her pocket to accept the scepter he handed over. "Thank you," she said.

"Are these important?" Parker asked Jane. "Why are they called honours?"

Her eyes flashed in the dim light. "Parker, the Honours are another name for all of this. We just found the Scottish Crown Jewels."

Epilogue

Glasgow, Scotland
2 weeks later

Not for the first time that day, Parker checked his rearview mirror, squinting against the sunlight. Empty road stretched behind the blue Mustang, but he still goosed the throttle. Anyone trying to follow them would have a hell of a task staying hidden and keeping up at the same time. His dog Tory voiced annoyance in the back seat as they rounded a sharp turn at speed.

"Easy, boy. We're almost there."

Jane reached back from the passenger seat and scratched behind Tory's ears, instantly becoming his new Favorite Person Ever. "It's a rough ride back there, isn't it, Mr. Tory?" His tail smacked the seat rapid-fire. "Are you sure Bertie's okay with you bringing Tory?" Jane said, turning back to Parker. "He has a dog too."

"Bertie said he'd be surprised if his pooch even wakes up. Apparently, the only thing it's on guard against is missing naps." A sign for Glasgow buzzed past and Parker pulled off the motorway and maneuvered into town, past pubs and homes older than the United States. The bumpy cobblestone streets gave the vehicle's suspension a serious test. "This will sound strange, but he sounded *excited* to tell us what happened."

Jane exhaled deeply. "At least somebody is willing to do it. The authorities didn't admit anything at all, even after my interview. You think they would show a little thanks considering what we found for them." She drank from a water bottle. "Even though revealing a government has been lying to its citizens for several hundred years is a delicate issue."

"Governments lie all the time," Parker said. "Only usually they don't have to own up to it."

"Perhaps they should have thought of that when they realized Scotland's Crown Jewels were lost several centuries ago. Staging a dramatic 'recovery'," here she flashed air quotes with both hands, "is not how to handle the matter."

"Whoever made those decisions is long dead. And think about it. If they'd caught James and retrieved the Crown Jewels, we wouldn't have been able to find them."

"At least I finally have a story to beat all of Hugh's old tales," Jane said. "Thank goodness he's okay. The doctors say he'll be good as new once his stitches come out in a few days."

"I'll raise a glass to that," Parker said. Actually, he hadn't raised many glasses of late, not since the showdown at Barnbougle Castle two weeks before. Narrowly avoiding an early death did wonders for personal resolve. Between police interviews and catching up on his investment business at home, he'd made it back to the gym, shed ten pounds, and cut the unmanageable hair he'd neglected for too many months. Jane had even commented on his vigorous appearance today when he'd picked her up.

Of course, they weren't the only ones who'd experienced a close shave from their research, and Bertie wanted to tell them about his troubles in person.

"I had no idea stonemasons did this much business." Parker whistled as he pulled into the only available parking spot in front of Bertie's workshop. "It's packed."

"Let's hope Bertie isn't disappointed in us," Jane said as she knocked on the front door. "I left my whiskey at home."

"Something tells me he keeps a bottle or two on hand." An aproned man let them in, then walked outside and closed the door behind him. On his way out, he turned the orange and black sign on the door to *Closed.*

"Have a seat, my young friends." Bertie smacked his cane on the floor. "And bring that furry fellow over here. We offer treats for canine visitors." Parker noted Bertie's dog asleep in the same place it had been during their last visit. He didn't even look when Tory trotted over and sniffed around for a moment before rejoining Parker. "Forgive me for not getting up," Bertie said. "Old men are permitted their indulgences."

Alone in the cavernous working garage, Parker and Jane joined Bertie around the same table as before, though this time the whiskey was already out alongside a lavish tea setting.

"Here, boy." Bertie rattled a tin box, which definitely got his dog's attention. "One for you," he tossed a treat to Tory, who snatched it out of mid-air, "and one for you." The treat tossed toward his dog was gobbled immediately.

"Thanks for inviting us," Parker said. "Jane and I haven't been able to get much out of the police since everything happened. All they did was ask a bunch of questions and tell us to keep everything to ourselves."

"Bloody bastards." Bertie's cane pounded the floor. "A lot of good they did for me. Protect the public?" One veiny hand waved through the air. "My arse. I took care of this myself. If it was up to them, I would be in the ground."

Parker poured a small measure of whiskey for himself.

"Fill up another," Bertie said, holding out his glass. "No good for a man to drink alone."

Jane accepted a glass as well. "As Parker said, the authorities didn't reveal much about what happened here in your shop." She took a drink and let the sentence hang.

"The men who came here learned about me from listening in on your place," Bertie said. The chair creaked as he settled back with his glass clasped between both hands. "What was it, a telephone company van?" Jane nodded. "Put a tap on your lines," Bertie said. "Heard our conversation, and then what Hugh said to you. The one who came here drove a phone company van. Not a real one, of course, just made to look the part."

"How long did it take them to get here after we left?" Jane asked.

Bertie shrugged. "Not sure. Could have been sitting on the place for hours. All I know is around six that evening, all my employees are gone, the shop is empty, and I'm in here. I check the books every night over there." He pointed to a desk in one corner. "Since you told me what happened, I had the shotgun with me."

"I thought it was under that chair." Parker pointed to Bertie's bottom.

"Man needs more than one shotgun." Bertie sipped his drink. "A telephone van pulled up out front. Hard to see my desk from where he parked, and the sign said Closed, so I sat. When he gets out, I don't like him."

"Why not?" Jane asked.

"If you need stone work done, you come to the store. This man stood there. And watched. That's all he did – looked at the store and the workshop. No man comes to a stonemason in a telephone van to look at the building. Bastard was up to no good and I knew it."

Tory returned from a search of the garage and settled at Parker's feet. "You didn't get worried?" Parker asked, scratching Tory's ears.

"Takes more than one to worry me. I've lived a long life, seen too much. A man learns when to worry after so many years." Bertie aimed his cane at the desk. "You have to prepare in life. Look at the front of the desk, right in the middle. Go over there and look hard, tell me what you see."

Parker crossed the open concrete floor and knelt in front of the desk. It took a few seconds, but he eventually spotted the faint circular outline right below the desktop. "Looks like you cut a hole out and then plugged the wood," Parker said when he sat back down. "What's it for?"

"To stick a shotgun barrel through."

Parker's jaw dropped a fraction. Jane's did more than that.

"Are you serious?" she asked.

"Better if they never see it coming," Bertie said. "He had a gun too, a pistol. Didn't know it at first. The man came inside and made his first mistake. Didn't ask who I was or where to find Robert Gray. He talked to me right off." Again, Bertie's hand waved. "Just a bit of nonsense to make sure I was alone and the shop was empty. Then he had a question about the stone. I said I didn't have anything to say and that he should go now. Then he made the second mistake." Sipping his drink, Bertie waited until Parker sat on the edge of his seat. "He showed me his pistol."

Jane was nearly falling off her chair. "And you shot him."

"What else would I do? Looking at the wrong end of a gun is no time to muddy about. I had my shotgun aimed when he walked in. Two barrels in the chest took the fight out of him. Knocked him back outside."

"What did you tell the police?" Jane asked.

"That I am a businessman who has dealt with burglars in the past. One who'd had enough. A man came through my door with a pistol. Lucky for me I had the shotgun." Bertie leaned forward, selected a biscuit after some deliberation. "The police understand. Don't like robbers at all, same as me."

This old guy was a Scottish John Wayne, thought Parker. "You don't really worry about what the police have to say, do you?" he asked.

"Haven't for a long time, young man. The sooner you learn to rely on yourself, the better." He ate the biscuit in one bite. "Now, I've talked enough. Tell me what you found at the end of all those old letters."

Jane hadn't wanted to discuss anything over the phone with Bertie, not after the issue with her tapped phone lines leading to Hugh's injury. The old stonemason had been content to wait for their arrival, aware only that the authorities had been all over Barnbougle Castle for a week straight and that Parker and Jane swore up and down they couldn't talk about any of it, at least until now.

"The government made us sign non-disclosure agreements," Jane said. "But I think we can trust you to keep a secret."

Bertie winked at her. "To the grave."

"You'd better. First, you have to realize I had no idea what we were after. James always called what he had *honours*, which led me to believe we were after a paper granting land or title. Something one person could carry around the country without drawing attention."

"Hugh actually solved it," Parker said. He detailed the picture of Hugh as a young boy, and the books he'd been reading before he was attacked. "The intruder snuck up on Hugh and bashed him over the head, then injected him with a sedative to knock him out."

A grin cracked Bertie's lined features. "Must have been strong to keep Hugh out cold."

"It was," Jane said. "Powerful stuff. Before they knocked him out, Hugh realized the last clue pointed to a castle. *Barnbougle Castle.* The home I grew up in was the *X* on James's map through Scotland."

Bertie was not impressed. "Makes sense. Your place is close to a city, and far enough away to avoid attention. James may have been from Edinburgh. He would have known of the castle." He reached for the whiskey and poured another glass, topping Parker up as well. "A castle is big enough to hide most anything if you find the right place."

When you put it that way, it sounded almost logical. "We have a mausoleum as well," Jane said. "That's where we found it."

Bertie sipped his whiskey. "Easy to get in and out after dark."

Jane shuddered slightly. "No thanks. That place is creepy enough during the day. We had to go to the very end, to the oldest graves. That's where they have been for over three hundred years." Jane reached into her pocket and pulled out a folded piece of paper. "This is what we found."

Bertie unfolded it to reveal a picture Jane had printed that morning, the one she'd taken of their find on her father's desk. "Bloody hell." The bushy white hedges above each eye threatened to fly off. "I recognize these." His eyes narrowed. "They keep them in Edinburgh Castle."

"That's what the government tells you," Jane said. "When did you start trusting them?"

"Fair point." Bertie set the paper down. "You found the Crown Jewels of Scotland with your dead ancestors." Jane nodded. "I recall they went missing a long time past, were lost for a century. These letters started about that time, did they not?" Again, she confirmed it. "This fellow James must have stolen the Crown Jewels. Any idea why?"

"We don't think it was just for money," Jane said. "You likely know Scottish Parliament was dissolved in 1707." Bertie nodded. "Scottish Parliament united with the English Parliament to become the Parliament of Great Britain. Until 1707 the crown jewels were used during Parliamentary sessions to signify the king or queen's consent to any Acts passed."

Parker jumped in. "Our guess is someone in England wanted to steal the jewels, to take them back to England even though they had been Scotland's all along. Another small way of showing England really called the shots, not Scotland."

"A fair guess," Bertie said. "James steals the crown jewels to protect Scotland's honor. Or honours, in this case."

"Correct," Jane said. "When he succeeded, no one in the English or Scottish government wanted to admit what happened."

"So the government lied to cover up the theft," Bertie said. "And after another hundred years, decided to lie again and say they found them."

Parker had read extensively on the subject during the past few weeks. "In 1818 a group of men claimed to have found them in a long-forgotten chest in Edinburgh Castle," he said. "What they found, or rather, what they *made,* were forgeries. Meant to hide the fact the government had lost their most famous possessions. Put the fake ones on public display, threaten anyone who knows the truth, and your problem is gone."

"Any crown or sword would serve," Bertie said. "Belief makes it true. As long as the people have faith, it doesn't matter if it is real."

"The current administration certainly wanted them back," Jane said. "I called the First Minister's office. Once I spoke to the right person, men in suits showed up at my home within the hour. The first thing they did was take the honours and both of us to a secure location."

Parker nodded. He had been furious, ready to walk out when the government officials had shown up. "We sat there forever," he said. "Then we went through about a thousand interviews, all of which led to us signing the thickest non-disclosure agreement I've ever seen. Basically, if we ever tell anyone about this, they can extradite me from America and throw both of us in jail until the end of time."

"That's not all they did," Jane said. "We received compensation for 'returning' the lost items."

Bertie grunted. "Those tight-fisted bastards actually paid you?"

"In a manner of speaking," Jane said. "They are establishing a scholarship in Hugh's name for my department. One student a year, forever." She smiled. "Hugh won't admit it, but I think he's touched."

"What about you?" Bertie asked, looking to Parker. "Anything for the American?"

"I don't need money, so I suggested the government waive property or transaction taxes on Barnbougle Castle and other White family properties in perpetuity."

"Did they?" Bertie asked. Parker told him they had, and the old man actually laughed. "Well done, young man. Stick it to those greedy bastards any chance you get."

"That was pretty much the end of it," Jane said. "We agree never to tell anyone about it, my department gets a permanent scholarship, and I never pay property taxes again. Oh, and they pay for Hugh to have the best medical care money can buy until he's better. All in all, a bargain for the government."

"And you make an old fellow like me happy today."

Bertie fell into silence, and Parker was content to join him. Jane didn't seem to mind either. Tory fell asleep, and for a time the only sound in Bertie's garage was the wind blowing softly outside. It all came to an end when Bertie tapped his cane on the ground twice in rapid succession.

"That's right, then."

Parker glanced at Jane. "What's right?" he ventured.

"Come with me." Without waiting for a response, Bertie heaved himself to his feet and walked across the room toward a display table. Parker noted he didn't use his cane at all. "Do you remember this?"

"How could we forget?" Jane laid a hand on the rock. "Your Stone of Scone replica."

"You never told the police about the message we found, did you?" Parker asked.

"No reason to." He pointed to Jane. "Do you remember how I put a message in the repaired Stone?"

She did. "What did it say?" Jane asked.

"Don't remember. I'm an old man. I forget things." The edges of his mouth may have curled up a bit, though it was hard to tell. "The break left a natural opening for the paper. The replica, though, that one's solid. Nothing inside."

Now Bertie touched a machine by the table, what looked like an old projector of sorts, the kind you used to see in classrooms. Except this one had a futuristic screen on it. "I use this to see the damage inside anything I fix. If I don't know where the weak spot is, I might make things worse."

"Like an X-ray," Parker said.

"Yes." He flipped a switch, and the machine hummed. "Put this on the rock and you can see inside." He handed Jane what looked like a vacuum extension, then tapped the digital screen. "On here."

When she set the viewing device on the rock, the interior flashed to life in three dimensions, all in varying shades of green. "Are these lighter parts more porous?" Jane asked.

"Yes, they're not as solid. Cracks or holes show up as dark lines."

Jane moved the viewer around, soon revealing a solid green line zig-zagging through the piece. "What's that?"

"A repair."

"An interior defect in the replica? That means it was damaged before you carved it."

"Look here." He touched the very center. "This will help you understand."

When she moved the viewer, a dark green line extended halfway down the screen, surrounded by the different shades of green they'd seen so far. Then a black circle appeared with a translucent square outlined in the very middle.

The handheld viewer clattered to the floor.

"That's what a missing piece in the inside of a stone looks like," Bertie said, patting the Stone of Scone. "A cavity with a message inside."

THE END

Author's Note

This story is a work of fiction, though most of the tale is based in fact. What parts? As some would say, the more interesting ones, of course. To begin with, the crown jewels, or "Honours". To start, the facts. The Scottish Crown Jewels exist and are the oldest surviving set of crown jewels in the British Isles. Three objects comprise the jewels; a crown, a scepter and a sword. They are currently on display in the Crown Room at Edinburgh Castle. How they came to reside there is a remarkable story.

Originally used for the coronation of Scottish monarchs beginning in 1543, the jewels also served to represent the approval, or assent, of the British monarchy to Scottish legislation passed by the Parliament of Scotland. This time period includes the jewels narrowly surviving an attempt by Oliver Cromwell to melt all the English Crown Jewels down into coins, an act which nearly succeeded. If it weren't for a quick smuggling act by a group of enterprising parish church officials during a siege laid by Cromwell's forces, the jewels would most likely be coins now. However, they dodged an old, round bullet and were eventually recovered after the Restoration in 1660. After this, though, the jewels were not used to crown any further Scottish sovereigns and took their place at the Parliament of Scotland.

All was well until the Acts of Union in 1707, which united the kingdoms of Scotland and England into the kingdom of Great Britain. With the Parliament of Great Britain sitting in London, the Scottish Crown Jewels were out of a job and were subsequently locked in a chest at Edinburgh Castle and completely forgotten about. Hard to believe, but it's true. They gathered dust until 1818 when a historian named Walter Scott and a handful of other officials were authorized by the soon-to-be George IV to knock down some royal Scottish walls and find the jewels. Lo and behold, the jewels were still in that same chest they'd been tossed in over a hundred years earlier.

In another twist of history that you would never suspect is true, the Stone of Scone (or Stone of Destiny, as it's also called) was actually stolen by a group of four Scottish students in 1950. These inept young thieves took the over three-hundred-pound block of sandstone from Westminster Abbey in London and promptly dropped it, breaking the stone in half. The bumbling group eventually buried the stone in a field for several weeks before taking it to a Glasgow stonemason for repairs. The stonemason? A man named Robert "Bertie" Gray. Bertie truly did put a paper message inside the repaired stone, though it was hidden inside a brass rod and to this day no one knows was what written on it, Bertie having taken the secret to his grave. Police eventually received a "tip" the Stone was left at Arbroath Abbey in Scotland, and they recovered the Stone, returning it to Westminster Abbey. In 1996 the British government determined the Stone would be kept in Scotland unless needed for a coronation, so the Stone can now be found in the Crown Room at Edinburgh Castle, alongside the crown jewels.

Barnbougle Castle is a real structure which stands today. It overlooks the Firth of Forth, and the now privately-owned castle truly has a legend associated with it regarding the impending death of Barnbougle's owner and a hound crying. The mausoleum in which Parker finds the lost jewels is my invention.

Robert the Bruce's heart is truly buried at Melrose Abbey. Visitors may view a plaque noting the heart on the abbey grounds.

The Stirling Heads medallions in Stirling castle are real, though any descriptions beyond size and basic carvings come from my imagination.

St. Salvator's chapel at St. Andrews is real, and is a center for student activities.

As a final aside, the hidden clues, notes and murderous tales are all created by the author. While Scotland's storied past is ripe for inventing wondrous tales of glory and deception, this tale is just that; a work of fiction meant to entertain and hopefully engage readers, leaving them wondering what is true and what is not. I encourage you to research these components to learn more about the past.

Above all, I hope you enjoyed reading this book as much as I enjoyed writing it.

GET THE ANDREW CLAWSON STARTER LIBRARY

FOR FREE

Sharing the writing journey with my readers is a special privilege. I love connecting with anyone who reads my stories, and one way I accomplish that is through my mailing list. I only send notices of new releases or the occasional special offer related to the Parker Chase or TURN series.

If you sign up for my mailing list, I'll send you a free copy of the first Parker Chase and TURN novels as a special thank you. You can get these books for free by signing up here:

DL.bookfunnel.com/L4modu3vja

Did you enjoy this book? Let people know

Reviews are the most effective way to get my books noticed. I'm one guy, a small fish in a massive pond. Over time, I hope to change that, and I would love your help. The best thing you could do to help spread the word is leave a review on your platform of choice.

Honest reviews are like gold. If you've enjoyed this book I would be so grateful if you could take a few minutes leaving a review, short or long, on this book's Amazon page.

Thank you very much.

Dedication

For the newest member of our family.

What a wonderful life it will be.

Also by Andrew Clawson

Have you read them all?

In the Parker Chase Series

A Patriot's Betrayal

A dead man's letter draws Parker Chase into
a deadly search for a secret that could rewrite history.
Free to download

The Crowns Vengeance

A Revolutionary era espionage report sends Parker
on a race to save American independence.

Dark Tides Rising

A centuries-old map bearing a cryptic poem sends Parker Chase
racing for his life and after buried treasure.

A Republic of Shadows

A long-lost royal letter sends Parker on a secret trail
with the I.R.A. and British agents close behind.

A Hollow Throne

Shattered after a tragic loss, Parker is thrust into
a race through Scottish history to save a priceless treasure.

In the TURN Series

TURN: The Conflict Lands

Reed Kimble battles a ruthless criminal gang

to save Tanzania and the animals he loves.

Free to download

TURN: A New Dawn

A predator ravages the savanna. To stop it, Reed must be

what he fears most – the man he used to be.

Check my website AndrewClawson.com for more details,

and additional Parker Chase and TURN novels.

About the Author

Andrew Clawson is the author of the Parker Chase and TURN series.

You can find him at his website, AndrewClawson.com, or you can connect with him on Twitter at @clawsonbooks, on Facebook at facebook.com/AndrewClawsonnovels and you can always send him an email at andrew@andrewclawson.com.

Made in the USA
Monee, IL
17 October 2020